USBORNE

Knitbone Pepper Ghost Dog

A Horse Called Moon

By Claire Barker Illustrated by Ross Collins

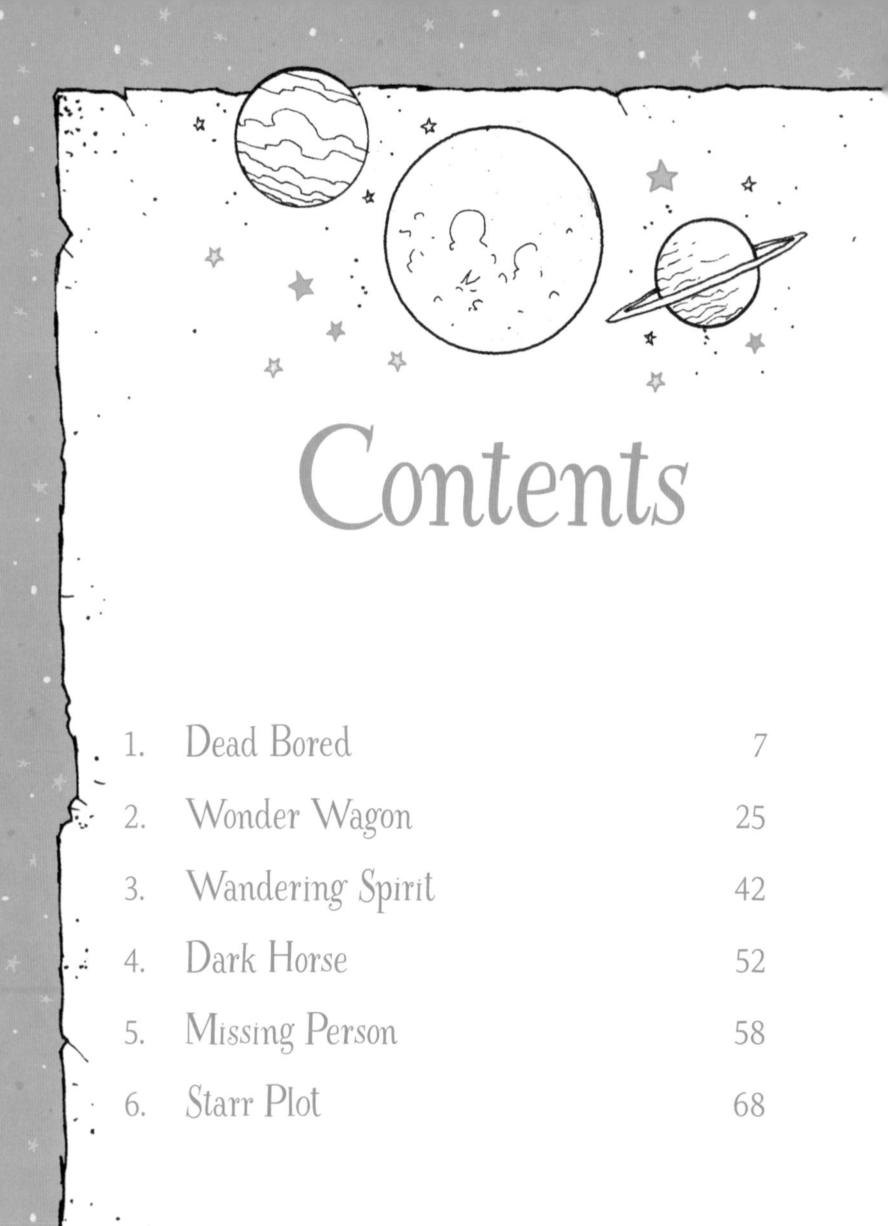

Contents

Chapter 1

Dead Bored

"I'm soooo booored," howled Knitbone Pepper, paws over his eyes. "Bored, bored, bored."

"Me too," moaned Martin the hamster, slashing his tiny sword back and forth in frustration. "I'm more *bored* than a bored thing."

It was a damp and drizzly Sunday morning, with rain trickling down the windowpanes, drop by drop. Orlando the monkey gave a huge yawn. He carefully selected a teaspoon from his handbag and banged his head with it.

Starcross Hall of Bartonshire, England, had shut its huge doors for the winter. So recently full of tourist squeals and laughter, the house had fallen into a deep slumber once more. Dust sheets had been hauled over the hat collections and the *Hats Off to Starcross* sign had been taken down. The cafe chairs were stacked and the souvenir shop was shut. The corridors yawned and the empty rooms dozed.

Lord and Lady Pepper, exhausted after such a busy summer season, had popped on their lavender-snooze eye masks, gone to their bedroom and had fallen, face down, into a deep sleep for days. Other than the tick-tock of the library clock, the whole house was quieter than the grave.

Valentine the hare gazed out of the window at the drifting autumn leaves, hoping he looked wistful and handsome. "It's strange without the visitors, isn't it?" he mused, brushing his long ears and arranging his whiskers artfully. "It's a bit spooky."

"I do miss the excitement," sighed Winnie Pepper in wonder, looking at a large, framed poster on the wall. "Did Circus Tombellini really come to Starcross, or was it just a brilliant dream?

It was so magical to see the old place come alive, even though it was only for the summer…"

Gabriel the goose flapped his wings impatiently and tutted. "Heavens to Betsy, everyone! The exhibition has only been shut for a week!" he honked, straightening the *Open Again in the Spring* sign on the hall window. "Honestly, the way you lot are going on you'd think someone had died! Geddit? DIED! It's a joke. It's funny, you see, because we're ANIMAL GHOSTS! Ha ha!"

But Knitbone didn't see the funny side. As he plodded up the steps to their attic, he thought to himself that a week without the exhibition already felt like for ever. It wasn't just the lack of visitors either. Winnie was back at school and he missed her all day long. It wasn't fair – he only saw her in the mornings. And in the evenings. And at weekends. And the time he spent staring at her whilst she slept. Aside from those times he hardly saw her at all.

It's not that he wasn't grateful to be a ghost – being a Beloved was the best thing ever – but the summer had been so much fun. At the top of the stairway he turned and howled. "But now there's nothing to do, Gabriel! Dogs need things to *do*!"

"Goodness gracious ME, Knitbone Pepper!" said Gabriel, waddling up the stairs behind him. "As both a Beloved *and* a member of the Spirits of Starcross, there's never any time to be bored! Being guardians of heart and home is very time-consuming. There are lots of jobs to do."

"Like what?" asked Martin sulkily, clambering onto the top step and eyeing the goose accusingly with his telescope.

"Well, you know…" said Gabriel, ruffling his wings defensively. "Lots of things, like…um… sorting socks…dusting…hoovering…"

Everyone groaned and Knitbone nudged the attic door open with his nose. Martin raced inside and promptly dived into a packet of comforting ginger nuts. After adventures with ghost tigers, circuses and international jewel thieves, the prospect of housework was duller than dishwater.

Swinging himself up onto an old packing case, Orlando reached out and unpinned the circus postcard from its place on the wall. It had a boy and a tiger on the front. He pressed his face to the picture and a tear rolled down his monkey cheek. "Orlando miss snaggletooth tigerface.

Orlando *love* him." He gave a little sniff. "Orlando *miss* him."

"We all miss Roojoo," sighed Knitbone. "Read the postcard again."

Orlando read it out, slowly, with dramatic pauses for sobs.

Dear Winnie, Knitbone, Gabriel,
Valentine, Orlando and Martin.
We are now in Germony. The gingerbread here is delicious and most energizing! I've been making new friends along the way.
I've bumped into a few more Beloveds.
As you say:
"A Beloved in need is a friend indeed!"
Word is getting about...
Miss you,
Love and hoops of fire
Roojoo xxxxx

14.9.
DEUCH

Winnie P
Starcr
Barto

There was a long, fed-up silence. Winnie reached into her pocket and took out the gift that Bertie, the circus ringmaster, had given her. Holding the beautiful pocket watch up in the autumn light, she read the inscription out loud: "Friendship is Timeless". She gave a small sigh and even Gabriel's good mood began to sag a little. The atmosphere hung limply in the air, like a day-old party balloon.

"I find, in challenging circumstances such as these," Gabriel parried, "that books can be very helpful." He reached for *The Good Ghost Guide*, which he had re-shelved in the Beloved's attic room for convenience.

"You're a librarian goose. You *always* think books are very helpful," sighed Knitbone, walking in a circle on the spot and plonking down, spreading out in a puddle of glum.

"That is because they *are*. And kindly remember, Knitbone Pepper, that this isn't any old book, it's THE book. We need something to keep us busy until the spring and this book will have the answer. For example," he said, his blue eyes twinkling, "there's a whole section on hobbies. That'll lift our spirits!" Gabriel flicked to the right page and jabbed a wing tip at it. "There! You see? Starting at A."

Knitbone looked down at the page and raised a doubtful eyebrow. "Armadillo Collecting? Ant Farming? What are you getting at, Gabriel?"

The goose tutted. "Not those, THAT one." He pointed to a different word.

Valentine spelled it out. "A-R-C-H-A-E-O-L-O-G-Y." He looked up and cocked his long ears to one side. "What's that?"

"That, my dear friend, is a hobby where you look in the ground for buried treasure." Gabriel's feathery chest puffed out, a sure sign he was about to say something clever. "The official term is an *archaeological dig.*"

Straight away, Knitbone's ears pricked up and he sprang to his feet. Dig? In the *dirt*? Now Gabriel was talking! Suddenly everything was starting to look up.

They went straight to the old conservatory. Once a sunny Victorian wonder, it had been left languishing in the dark for nearly a century. Now it looked like a gloomy sunken ship, palm trees towering towards the glass ceiling like wonky masts. It was a secret garden, where all sorts of plants had been allowed to run wild; twisting and rambling unchecked, creating a thick jungle of strange blossoms and fruits. Rich in rubbish and junk, experience had taught Knitbone that it would be the ideal spot for a bit of treasure hunting.

A few years earlier he and Winnie had found a priceless dinosaur bone in there and nearly sent it to the Natural History Museum – until Lady Pepper had gently pointed out that it was, in fact, just a lamb chop.

Moving the old black and white floor tiles, Valentine used his powerful back legs to dig big holes and Gabriel used his beak to rifle about in the dirt. They quickly found precious pennies and a few muddy pieces of jigsaw. Martin was covered in so much soil that he looked just like a little potato.

Orlando, using a spoon from Lady Pepper's old handbag, carefully unearthed a smooth, round object.

He gasped and held it aloft. "Eez a mushroom made of ancient woodenness!" he breathed, full of wonder, his round eyes shining.

"No it's not, you noodle," said Martin flatly, inspecting the object. "It's a doorknob. Keep digging."

By the end of the morning they had quite a hoard of treasure/rubbish. Coloured bottles, pieces of plates, ring pulls and broken tiles were piled up in a wobbly tower. Gabriel recorded them all on his clipboard. Martin dug up a tiny toy soldier and Orlando unearthed a blue plastic owl. Overcome with emotion, he lovingly christened it "Twit", and swore to love it for ever.

Knitbone spent most of the morning with his nose down a particular hole, snuffling, snorting and digging. He got very excited, thinking he might have found a sword or at the very least a giraffe bone, but in the end it just turned out to be a thing that looked like a bit of old drainpipe. It was most disappointing.

"What have you got there, Knitbone?" asked Winnie, wiping her muddy hands on her knees.

Knitbone carried it over and plonked it at her feet.

Winnie picked it up and looked carefully at it.

It wasn't a pipe, because it had glass in both ends.

"Knitbone, you clever old thing," said Winnie, peering through one grubby end and laughing in surprise. "I think you've found some sort of telescope."

Knitbone wagged his tail. He didn't think that a telescope was anywhere near as exciting as a giraffe bone, but if Winnie was pleased then he was pleased.

"Aha!" honked Gabriel, his beak covered in mud like badly applied lipstick. "Good work, Knitbone. Perfect timing in fact, as the next hobby in the book is – Astronomy! Studying the stars!" He flapped his wings in excitement. "To the library!"

The Beloveds obediently trooped out of the conservatory and along the corridor, leaving a trail of muddy footprints. They were ready to get stuck into the reference books.

And *get stuck in* was exactly what Winnie did, rather like glitter to glue.

Knitbone knew she was the cleverest girl in the whole world, but even *he* was surprised by her sudden hunger for all things astronomical. From that Sunday afternoon on she gobbled up books on supernovas and black holes like they were cupcakes, reaching for another before she'd finished the last one. Winnie read and read, devouring and scoffing and stuffing her brain with information as if she couldn't get enough. She gushed about spiral galaxies and raved about the wonders of cosmic snowballs. From dawn until dusk she pondered dark matter, flare stars and space dust.

The others, slightly alarmed and not quite so captivated, briskly moved on from the As to the Bs, which meant Basket-weaving, Bowling in the Ballroom and Being Bored. But Winnie Pepper only had eyes for the stars.

Chapter 2
Wonder Wagon

One October evening, a few weeks later, Knitbone was on the front step, enjoying the light from a ginger biscuit moon, when a peculiar rush of wind whipped up. It barrelled down the lane and into the courtyard, shaking the trees, swirling and whirling the autumn leaves in cinnamon spirals. He raised his doggy nose and gave a deep, long sniff, breaking the scent down into its different parts. Like all dogs, Knitbone was very good at smells. This wind was very interesting;

a mysterious mixture of woodsmoke, grass and leather. It smelled of news. It smelled of secrets.

Knitbone stretched and let out a huge yawn: interesting smells or not, it was time for bed. As he climbed the long sweeping staircase, he was vaguely aware of a grim shadow wobbling in a dark, cobwebby corner. Mrs Jones, a grumpy ghost spider known as a Bad Egg, was teetering on the edge of her vase in the downstairs hallway. As usual she shook her spidery fist at him and glared in a vengeful manner. But on this particular evening, Mrs Jones was wasting her time and wouldn't get so much as a tiny growl out of Knitbone.

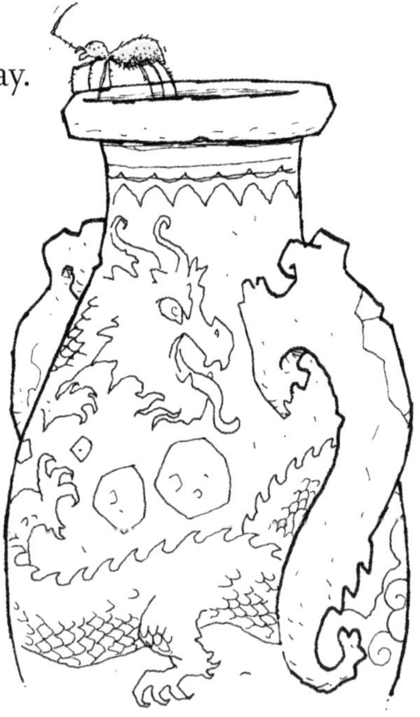

This evening, Knitbone was in extremely high spirits because tomorrow was the day he'd been waiting weeks for – the first day of the autumn half-term holiday.

Knitbone didn't approve of school, mostly because Winnie had to leave him behind. Being a Beloved was dead brilliant, but it meant being tied to your home for ever – in his case, the Starcross Estate. As a consequence, Knitbone couldn't go any further than the bus stop.

His heart brimming, Knitbone leaped up the last few steps. Nine whole days with his wonderful Winnie – NINE WHOLE DAYS! Nothing was going to get in the way of a mood this good, not even a Bad Egg.

As Knitbone skidded into the bedroom he could see the other ghosts were draped across Winnie's cosy rug; reading books and winding down to bedtime. The nights were drawing in and it got dark much earlier than in the summertime.

By now the Beloveds were nearly halfway through the alphabetical list of hobbies and had spent an exhausting day Jumping, Juggling Jam Jars and Joining Jigsaws.

Winnie, still stuck firmly on "A for Astronomy", sat in her pyjamas at her window, her eye pressed to the telescope. An ever-growing pile of reference books formed a small mountain next to her bed.

"The sky over Starcross is truly incredible. It's like tiny diamonds have been spilled all over the night," she said. "And I can see things so much better through this. Knitbone Pepper, you really are a clever dog."

Knitbone had tried to learn about astronomy, he really had, but the truth was he found it all a bit difficult. He'd read books about it in the library, but remembering everything was rather hard. It was like trying to hold onto slippery jelly snakes. He much preferred to read about squirrels. You knew where you were with squirrels.

"Look!" exclaimed Winnie, pointing at a silver splash of light streaming across the night sky. "A shooting star! In olden days that used to mean that visitors were coming."

"Fibby-foo stars," sighed Orlando, shaking his head. "Not until the spring has sprung."

Winnie continued, her eye scanning the heavens. "Look! Over there is Sirius the Dog Star! Did you know that it's part of the constellation Canis Major and it's the brightest star in the night sky? Or that there are lots of constellations named after animals? They are all listed in *The Night Sky* book over there, in case anyone wants to look." Winnie sighed happily. "Oh look! Over there is Pegasus the winged horse, the seventh largest of all of the constellations." She gazed up into the night sky. "There's a whole zoo of animals up there, you know: a lion, a peacock, a swan and lots of others too."

"Animals? A zoo?
Are there hamster stars?"
Martin jumped up and down like a bouncing ball. "Ooh! Ooh! I want to see the stars, too! Can I *please*, Winnie?" He pointed at his utility belt and shrugged matter-of-factly. "Only *my* telescope's got biscuit crumbs in it."

Winnie smiled and lifted the little hamster up to the eyepiece. He wiggled the telescope about, struggling to see. "Well I have to say this old contraption isn't much better than mine. I can't see any stars up there at all," he complained impatiently, changing its angle. "But there's some down *there*."

"What are you talking about?" asked Winnie. Martin pointed into the yard.

Everyone piled into the window alcove and looked down. There in the courtyard, bathed in starlight and swaying slightly in the wind, stood a rickety, rackety wooden wagon.

Knitbone leaped forwards with a jolt. *THAT wasn't there earlier*, he thought, lowering his shaggy eyebrows. *INTRUDERS!* He squashed his nose against the window. How exciting! This was definitely a Big Bark situation. Ever protective, Knitbone began to woof and bounce about the room, as if he had a bad case of angry hiccups.

"Calm down, Knitbone, you're overreacting as usual. It's just an old caravan," muttered Gabriel, craning his neck to see. "They must be lost."

With its back to the house, they could see that the wagon was painted a peeling dark blue and covered with fading glimmers of silver.

"Look what it says!" trilled Winnie with delight. A painted sign arched across the top. "*Moon and the Starrs*!"

Gabriel tutted and tapped his dictionary with a wing tip. "One thing's for sure. Whoever they are they're not very good at spelling. Even Martin knows there's only one 'r' in 'star'."

"Oi!" Gabriel received a sharp, hamstery kick in the knee.

"How wonderful!" said Winnie, hurriedly pulling on her dressing gown and slippers. "Maybe the owners are inside."

"They probably don't realize that the hat exhibition is closed for the winter," yawned Valentine. "We should tell them that they can come back in the spring."

The Beloveds trotted down the sweeping staircase and opened the front door. Winnie stepped out into the windy night, her pyjama legs and dressing gown whipping round her bare ankles. She looked left and then right, but the caravan had disappeared into the night.

"Where's it gone?" Winnie said.

"How strange," honked Gabriel. "It's a very big thing to suddenly vanish."

Orlando wagged his little finger wisely and

winked. "Maybe it was a dream. Maybe we is *ALL* mad as monkeys."

"Speak for yourself," said Martin, popping up out of Winnie's pocket and looking pointedly at Orlando. "I saw it clear as day. Nor am I mad, unlike *some* ghosts I could mention." His tummy rumbled loudly. "More to the point, is anyone else starving hungry?"

Knitbone's nose was already stuck to the floor, snuffling and truffling, hoovering scent along an invisible path. There was that smell again, the one he'd smelled earlier, only it was much stronger this time.

"What is it, boy?" said Winnie. "What can you smell?"

"Woodsmoke, grass, silver…and ginger. Definitely ginger. It was…*sniff*…here…and then…*snuffle*…it was over here…but…" He suddenly stood up, nose pointed, one paw lifted in the air, his tail horizontal. "Follow me!"

Knitbone trotted out of the courtyard, round the hedge and into the frosty darkness.

"Follow that doggy detective!" said Valentine. Winnie grabbed a torch and her wellies from the hall and they were off.

They would have made a peculiar sight, a dog sniffing and snortling a wiggly path around Starcross, closely followed by a torch-lit parade of ghostly animals and a girl in a dressing gown.

Knitbone took them on a merry dance up the lane, across to the bridge, over to the woods, back down to the vegetable garden, around the barn and back into the courtyard.

"Are you sure you know what you're doing, Knitbone?" asked Gabriel, looking up at the house doubtfully. "Only we seem to be back where we started."

"Shush, Gabriel," said Martin, adjusting his utility belt. "Tracking is an art. I've read about it in Combat Comics."

He pointed the tip of his sword at the goose, one eye shut. "A dog's nose never lies."

Suddenly, Knitbone stopped and

lifted up his nose. He took a long, deep sniff, drinking in the frosty air. "THE INTRUDER," he said, with a decisive bark, "IS IN THE ORCHARD!"

Martin was right: a dog's nose never lies. Two minutes later they were gathered around the back of the caravan, parked in the sparkling, frosty orchard.

Sprinkled with faded, painted stars, the wagon was something of a sad sight close up, splintered and tatty and wonky.

"Helloooo?" said Winnie, knocking gently on the back window.

"I don't think anybody's in," whispered Knitbone.

"Yes. Hello?" A female voice came from the front of the caravan, making them all jump. "Who's there?"

Bone-white and glowing in the starlight, a magnificent horse stood harnessed to the caravan.

Her shimmering mane cascaded down in loose snowy tresses. Her feet were trimmed with white feathery fluff, dusted with frost, and small twinkling silver bells hung from her bridle. She was bewitchingly beautiful. She was also rather wispy around the edges and most definitely, absolutely and *certainly* a ghost.

The horse whinnied softly, gazing at them with her pale blue eyes. "Good evening. Does anyone know where I might find Knitbone Pepper?"

MOON and the

Chapter 3

Wandering Spirit

Knitbone looked up at the horse and decided that she was not An Intruder. She looked nice, not at all like a cat or a suitcase. He knew he liked her straight away and dogs are always right about these sorts of things.

"Hello," he woofed politely. "*I'm* Knitbone Pepper. Welcome to Starcross."

The horse neighed with relief, her silver bridle bells jingling. "Are you? Are you *really*? Oh how wonderful! I've been all over the Starcross Estate but didn't expect to bump into you so soon!" She took a deep breath to slow herself down. "Forgive me," she breathed. Her voice was soft and musical. "I should introduce myself properly. My name is Moon Starr."

Having excellent manners, Knitbone held up a paw. "Nice to meet you, Moon," he said. Surprised that the others hadn't said anything, he turned around to look at them. "I *said* it's nice to meet her, *isn't it*, everyone?"

But Gabriel, Valentine, Orlando and Martin were stuck to the spot, tongue-tied and staring. Orlando's eyes seemed to be swimming about in their sockets, like dizzy goldfish. Martin was giggling like an idiot. The air filled with a mighty minty whiff.

Knitbone frowned. What on earth was wrong with them?

Winnie smiled and whispered into Knitbone's ear. "The peppermint blushing is a bit of a giveaway, don't you think? They've never met a girl ghost before."

Proving the point, Valentine and Gabriel gawped hopelessly. Orlando wrapped his tail around his eyes like a blindfold whilst Martin sucked his tummy in and tried to look tall.

Knitbone shook his head in despair and turned back to their new friend. "Anyway. So. Moon. How can we help?"

"Well," Moon explained, looking about furtively and lowering her voice to a whisper. "It's rather a long story. I was hiding behind a large rhododendron bush in London's Hyde Park, minding my own business, when a big tent appeared out of nowhere. From where I was standing, peeking though the branches, I could see a sign that said *Tombellini's Circus*. It was such a beautiful tent: reds and yellows, little flags. So when night fell, I thought I'd have a peek inside and—"

"Let me guess," interrupted Knitbone, one eyebrow raised. "Was there a ghost tiger inside? Very friendly? Big teeth? Size of a car?"

"Roojoo!" squealed Orlando in delight, peeking out from behind his tail.

Moon looked pleased as could be. "Yes! That's right!" In Moon's excitement, her words began to tumble over each other. "He explained that he was a Beloved, and then I realized that I must be one too – most illuminating. He was very kind. I asked if I could stay with the circus but he said that what I really needed to do was come and find you. He gave me a bag of German gingerbread and pointed me in the direction of Starcross. Roojoo said you were the best Beloveds anyone could hope to meet. He told me all about you and Winnie and the hats and his friend, Bertie, and the jewel robber. He said if anyone could help me, then it would be you!" She took another deep breath and lowered her head. "I'm sorry, I'm gabbling. It's just that I'm *so* glad to have found you."

"Hang on a minute," said Winnie. "Did you just say you were *hiding*?"

Moon looked instantly spooked, showing the whites of her eyes. Her ears twitched ticklishly and she began to dance nervously on the spot.

"Whoa there, Moon." Winnie stroked the horse's long white mane. "It's alright. You're safe here. At Starcross a Beloved in need is a friend indeed, aren't they, Knitbone?"

Knitbone nodded his head. "We're here to help you. Are you missing your person?"

"Yes." Moon gazed upwards through her

long lashes. "That is right, Knitbone Pepper."

"So where is your person then?" asked Knitbone, his head on one side, scratching one ear with his back foot.

At this point, all of the *oomph* seemed to go out of Moon. She slowly swayed her head back and forth and gave a long, deep sigh that seemed to come all the way from the bottom of her huge feathered feet.

"Well, that's the problem, you see. I don't know."

"Oh dear," said Knitbone, looking at the others. This *was* a problem. At least they had known where Winnie and Bertie were.

"The trouble is I lost her a very long time ago," said Moon. "I've always hoped that one day I might catch sight of her, perhaps by a road or in a wood, but I never have. I've been looking for seventy long years." She dropped her head down low. "The truth is I don't even know if she's still alive. I was hoping you could help."

Moon made soft whickering noises and pawed at the ground.

"Poor horse," said Winnie, gently stroking Moon's silky ears. "What's your person called?"

"Her name is Rosabel Starr," said Moon, "of the travelling family Starrs. It's spelled with an extra 'r', just like the sign says."

Martin blew a triumphant little raspberry at Gabriel.

Moon looked over her shoulder. "This caravan was our home, or what's left of it anyway. I'm afraid it's past its best." She cast her baleful blue eye over the ramshackle wagon, at its wobbly wheels and peeling paintwork. Even the lamps on the front had cracks in them and the curtains hung ragged and limp in the windows.

Knitbone let out a whimper. Poor Moon. He turned around.

"Martin – special emergency biscuit, please." Martin climbed into Winnie's pocket and reluctantly handed over the remains of a fluff-covered ginger cream.

"Now, now. It's not so bad. Don't be sad," said Knitbone, offering Moon the special biscuit.

"But it *is* bad, Knitbone Pepper," whinnied Moon anxiously, her eyes scanning the horizon, munching her biscuit. "It's very, *very* bad. I haven't even told you the really awful part yet." Her bottom lip quivered like jelly as she confessed: "I'm on the run."

"On the run?" Knitbone looked up at Winnie, wide-eyed. "What does that mean?"

"*On the run* means that she has escaped from someone, is that right, Moon?" said Winnie, her brow knotting in concern. This was all starting to sound rather worrying.

"Yes, Winnie Pepper, I'm afraid so." A tear rolled down Moon's long velvety nose.

"But who would be chasing a ghost horse?" asked Knitbone, feeling very confused.

Moon dropped her voice to a breathy whisper. "Can you keep a secret?"

"Of course!" everyone chimed, looking over their shoulders. Hugely intrigued, they leaned in close.

Moon looked about nervously. "Well, you know that we are *animal* ghosts?"

"*Yeeees.*"

"And you know there are *other sorts* of ghosts?"

"*Yeeees.*"

"Well…I'm hiding from a human one."

Chapter 4

Dark Horse

You could have knocked the Beloveds over with a feather. They'd never met a human ghost. Starcross only had animal ghosts, which was why it had such a nice, helpful atmosphere (with the exception of Mrs Jones, but she was a Bad Egg, not a Beloved, so she didn't count).

All they knew about human ghosts was what *The Good Ghost Guide* told them, and it wasn't very good. According to the book, human ghosts were terrible show-offs, interested in frightening everybody just for the sake of it. It would seem that this particular human ghost came with a whole host of other problems too.

"His name's Galloping Jasper," sighed Moon, rolling her eyes, "and he's a highwayman. He's 264 years old and he's an absolute nightmare."

"A highwayman?" Knitbone let out a fretful whine. "A scary olden days robber with a cloak and a mask?"

"Yes," said Moon, lowering her lashes in shame.

"But I thought highwaymen were supposed to have their own horses," asked Winnie, thinking about her storybooks.

"When he was alive he had a horse, but he never fed her properly, or stroked her ears," explained Moon. "Her shoes were always worn out and he galloped her to exhaustion. She was no more than a bag of bones at the end." She gave a little shiver. "They died in a duel with another highwayman and her spirit was set free. Jasper never saw her again, so there was something of a vacancy."

"What do you mean?" asked Knitbone. "A vacancy?"

"I mean a ghost highwayman needs a ghost horse. He found me wandering about in the wood not long after I became a spirit. You can imagine my horror when he moved into the caravan, saying it was a perfect home for a highwayman. He said that after years of holding up stagecoaches, he fancied a wagon for himself. He even insists on calling me the same name as his old horse – Black Bertha. It's all very upsetting."

"He sounds really frightening," squeaked Martin, clutching his chubby cheeks in dismay.

"Haven't you tried to escape before?" asked Valentine, round-eyed with horror and wringing his ears anxiously.

"Oh yes, many times, but he always found me again." Moon gave them a rueful glance. "I wouldn't wish him on my worst enemy." She looked around and dropped her voice to a tiny whisper. "One night he was visiting some of his old cronies in London – robbers, pickpockets and the like – and I saw my chance. He hadn't tied me up properly, you see, so I made a run for it. I kept galloping until I saw the sign for Hyde Park, as I knew it would be full of hiding places. Meeting Roojoo was such a stroke of luck."

Suddenly, a wolf whistle pierced the night like an arrow, making everyone jump.

"That'll be my mum," explained Winnie, half-apologetically. "We have to go, but we'll be back tomorrow." Winnie looked around at the orchard in the cold moonlight. "You'll be safe here tonight. Have you got everything you need?"

"Oh yes," said Moon politely, munching her biscuit and smacking her lips. She shrugged her shoulders and unhooked herself from the harness with a jingle. "I have to stay close to home of course, but it's nice to have a bit of a stretch at the end of the day."

Moon shook her long mane and let out a deep sigh of relief. "This is perfect. I'm always happiest free in the open air. Home is where you park it!" She felt the grass beneath her hoofs and looked up at the stars that peeked between the boughs above her head. "Such a hidden heaven. Roojoo was right; he said I would be safe in your paws. Thank you, Beloved friends."

The gang wandered out of the orchard,

crunched back across the gravel and climbed the stairs to bed.

"Goodness," said Winnie. "The holidays are turning out to be an adventure already!"

Knitbone's tail wagged so hard he felt like it might drop off.

Later that evening, Knitbone lay in the darkness of the wardrobe, his mind buzzing with thoughts. This really was a turn-up for the books. He mulled Moon's problems over and over, as the others fell into a restless sleep, their dreams filled with galloping ghosts and starry skies.

Chapter 5

Missing Person

The next morning, everybody sat in the kitchen as usual, Lady Pepper dishing up ladles of organic hedge porridge. It had quite a lot of fibre in it and was something of a jaw workout. This gave Winnie plenty of time to casually mention the caravan that had turned up in the orchard the previous night.

Most normal parents would be amazed, shocked or agog. They might be bewildered, suspicious or even flabbergasted. But Winnie's parents were not normal. They never seemed to bother about ordinary things, like the collapsing roof or the buzzard nesting in the shoe cupboard, so the sudden appearance of a caravan on the Estate was nothing to worry about. Still, Winnie didn't want her parents to find it and turn it into a makeshift honey pantry or hat warehouse.

"A caravan, you say?" said Lord Pepper, absent-mindedly picking bits of shrubbery from between his teeth and reading the morning paper. "Do you mean like the one that goes behind a car? For jolly holidays?"

"No, this is the sort you live in. It's painted," said Winnie. "And wooden. Can I use it as a den?"

"Oh!" squealed Lady P in delight, trying to prise the ladle out of the now-stiff porridge. "Do you mean a horse-drawn Romany caravan? How scrumptious! Yes of course, that sounds like an excellent idea. Every child needs a den." She turned to her husband. "Now, more delicious hedge porridge, dear? Or perhaps a pot of nettle tea?"

And that was that. The deal was done and dusted at the drop of a hat, just as Winnie had known it would be. The ghosts finished their game of snakes and ladders under the table and

followed Winnie out into the ballroom. Their plan to help Moon was about to take flight.

"Right," said Winnie, clapping her hands. "First things first." In the furthest corner of the ballroom was the Starcross computer. Lord and Lady Pepper had bought it when the hat exhibition first took off. It rarely got used though, as Lord Pepper couldn't get the hang of it. He said the very thought of it filled his head with angry bees. Blowing a blanket of dust away, Winnie sat down and turned on the computer.

"What are you going to do, Winnie?" yawned Knitbone curiously. He'd hardly slept a wink and technical matters were not his strength. Knitbone was good at practical things, like digging and howling at the bin man.

"I'm going to do an internet search," said Winnie, carefully entering the password MADASAHATTER. "We do searches at school all the time. The first thing we should do is find Moon's person. Rosabel Starr is quite an unusual name so there can't be that many of them."

Knitbone wagged his tail. This was much better than any of his ideas. He felt a warm glow of pride rise up from his paws to the tip of his nose. Knitbone turned to Gabriel and whispered, "she's looking at wobble sites. Skiing the net. I've seen it on television." He winked knowingly. "I told you she's the most brilliant girl in the world, didn't I?"

"Yes," said Gabriel with a knowing look, catching Valentine's eye. "You *have* mentioned it once or twice."

"Hooray! I've think I've found her!" said Winnie, her face lit up by the screen. "She lives in Holland, in a florist's." Her brow furrowed. "Oh, hang on a minute, she's twenty years old. That's no good."

Winnie tapped at the keyboard some more. "What about her?" Valentine pointed at the screen, where a black-and-white photograph of a strict-looking governess had appeared. It said *Rosabel Starr, born 1930, died 2010.*

"Died?" gasped Martin, his (third) breakfast biscuit halfway to his mouth.

"Oh no!" gasped Gabriel, covering his eyes with his wings. "We're too late! Poor Moon!"

"WOE, WOE AND THRICE WOE!" wailed Orlando, pulling a black sock over his head.

“Hold your horses,” mumbled Winnie, scrolling down. “Listen, it says here: *Miss Rosabel Starr lived in Texas, USA, all her life. She died of a terrible allergy to animal hair.*” Winnie turned to the Beloveds and scratched her head. “Well, that can’t be her.”

Determined not to give up, Winnie searched again, this time typing in *R Starr*. Straight away the University of the North Pole’s home page popped up, featuring a photograph of a very old lady next to an enormous telescope and an igloo. Winnie squealed in excitement, clasping her hands to her mouth.

Dr R Starr

Prizewinning astronomer and author,
Dr Starr is a scientist who has won many awards for her research. She spends her life travelling the world, seeking out the darkest skies.

Contact:

drstarr@universityofthenorthpole.snow

"Wow!" breathed Winnie, clapping her hands. "I really hope that's her! An actual real-life astronomer!"

"Do you think it is?" asked Valentine, squinting at the picture. "It doesn't say her name is Rosabel. It could be Rachel, or Rita."

"Or Ronald," said Martin, trying to be helpful.

Knitbone looked very carefully at the screen. This R Starr had kind eyes; the sort of eyes that animals trusted. He hoped it was her too.

Winnie pressed *print* and a copy of the photo juddered slowly out of the printer. "There's only one way to tell for sure." She whipped it up and made for the door. "Let's go and ask Moon."

Chapter 6

Starr Plot

Moon stood patiently in the orchard, sniffing the windfall apples. Hearing the other Beloveds approach, her soft ears flicked up to attention.

"Good morning, Moon!" woofed Knitbone.

"Hello there," chirped Winnie.

"Good morning, dear friends!" Moon whinnied, swishing her waterfall tail. "How are you all today?"

Orlando, Martin, Gabriel and Valentine

giggled shyly. The air was suddenly full of peppermint again.

Valentine was the first to pull himself together, standing up tall and smoothing his ears down. He gave a deep bow and cleared his throat. "Ahem. I bid thee a thousand good mornings, fair maiden."

Gabriel, sensing competition, hastily elbowed the hare out of the way. "Felicitations of the dawn, dear lady."

Knitbone, rolling his eyes in exasperation, pressed on. "Moon, let's get straight to the point." Winnie unrolled the piece of paper and held it up so that Moon could see. "Brace yourself. Is THIS the person you've been looking for?"

Moon stared at the photograph. Her nostrils flared and her jaw dropped in amazement. For a moment she couldn't say anything, lost for words. Then suddenly she let out a loud, joyful whinny.

"Oh my goodness! Yes! HER! YES! That's her!" She did a little excited tap dance on the spot.

"Oh how clever you are!
How did you do this so quickly?
To think I've been looking for years and *years* and *years* and you found her just like that. Roojoo said you would know what to do and he was right! Oh joy! Oh wonder of wonders!"

"Now, Moon, be sensible for a moment. Are you absolutely sure?" said Winnie seriously, trying to keep the excitement out of her voice. "She's probably changed quite a lot in those seventy years."

With some difficulty, Moon calmed herself down. She snuffled her nose all over the picture, making it rather damp, then gazed adoringly at it. "She might be an old lady now, with crinkly-wrinkles and snowy-white hair, but I would still know my precious Rosabel anywhere." Moon let out a sudden gasp, her eyes wide. "And look! LOOK at that! *She's still wearing my bell!*"

They all leaned in to look at the photograph. It was true. The old lady had a small, silver bell around her neck. "You see?" said Moon, shaking her head and tinkling brightly. "It's from my bridle! She unhooked it when she was a child and hung it around her neck, so that we would jingle in perfect time as we trotted along." Knitbone looked up at Moon's bridle. On close inspection there was indeed a little space where a bell should be, like a gap in a row of twinkly teeth.

"She hasn't forgotten me after all!" Moon let out a long, blissful sigh.

Feeling bold, Martin stepped forward and saluted, standing on tiptoe. "Martin Pepper at your service, ma'am. Begging your pardon, I don't want to chuck a spanner in the works, but we have a small issue. What Orlando would refer to as a 'podlob', so to speak."

Moon bent her long neck, her eyes meeting Martin's. "Spanners? Podlobs? What is this podlob? What are you talking about, little mouse?" Gabriel and Valentine sniggered.

"The podlob…ahem, I mean *problem*, ma'am, is that this Dr Rosabel Starr lives at the North Pole," he said, thrusting his little barrel chest out importantly. "That is to say, she lives at the far end of the world."

"THE NORTH POLE?" Moon looked at the picture again, noticing the igloo for the first time. Her blue eyes filled with dismay. "But that's so far away! What's she doing there?"

"She's an istroomier, ma'am," announced

Martin in his most authoritative tone.

"Oh. Oh no. That IS a podlob." Moon gave her tail a troubled swish and quickly slipped back into her harness. "Well then, I'd better head off straight away, I suppose. The journey of a thousand clips begins with the first clop. There's no time to lose. Soon I'll be near her once more! Farewell, dear friends, and thank you for your help." She gave her harness a jingle and broke into a brisk trot.

"Hang on a minute!" barked Knitbone, calling after her. "Don't rush off! Don't you want to be reunited with your person? I thought that's why you'd come to Starcross."

The caravan screeched to a halt, quickly moving into reverse. Moon looked back over her shoulder and stared at Knitbone for a long, disbelieving moment. "I beg your pardon?"

Knitbone cocked his head to one side in surprise. "Didn't Roojoo tell you about reuniting? Didn't he tell you about the special rules?"

Moon frowned as she tried to remember. "Well, we didn't have much time for the details. I was in something of rush."

"Reuniting," Knitbone explained slowly, "is where a Beloved and their living person are joined together again. Like me and Winnie, and Roojoo and Bertie."

Moon looked thoroughly bamboozled. Then

her thoughts began to click together, one by one. "Are you saying," she murmured, her eyes widening, "that Rosabel and I can be together again? Together-together? In a togethery way?"

"Yes," Knitbone woofed. "She'll even be able to see you! But reuniting only works at Starcross. You can't do it anywhere else."

Moon began to snort and stamp her feet in excitement. This was huge news. The caravan rocked on its wheels and even more bits fell off.

"Woah there, girl," soothed Winnie with a big grin. "Settle down or there'll be nothing left for Rosabel to come back home to!"

"First things first, though. We need to get Rosabel here!" said Knitbone.

"But how?" wondered Winnie. "We can't just email her and say, *hello, you don't know us but we've got your ghost horse*. She'll think we're bonkers."

Moon swung her head from side to side in

confusion. "This is simply too much for my horse brain. I don't know what to do!"

Horses, whilst noble and striking, are not actually that good at puzzles. Dogs, however, *are* and Knitbone could feel an idea bubbling up in his brain. They needed a plan.

Knitbone Pepper loved spending long summer afternoons lying in the fields, trying to catch bumblebees. He had learned that the best way to attract one of the buzzy fuzzy-humbugs was with a bright flower. But Rosabel was a person, not a bumblebee. What sort of bloom would attract an astronomer? He pondered the problem. Knitbone remembered Winnie's passion for the night sky and how pleased she'd been with the telescope. What was it Winnie had said? "*The sky over Starcross is truly incredible… Knitbone Pepper, you really are a clever dog.*"

In the distance, over by the vegetable garden, Knitbone could hear the buzzing of a chainsaw as

Lady Pepper gathered ingredients for dinner. Suddenly a thinking sum burst forth into his doggy brain.

He kicked a space in the dirt, grabbed a stick in his mouth and began to write.

"Knitbone, you're a barking genius!" cried Winnie. "That sounds brilliant! But how can we be sure that Rosabel will come?"

"Easy," woofed Knitbone, prancing happily about on the spot. "We could invite her to be the guest of honour, and make a big speech at the banquet. She is 'prizewinning' after all!"

"And we could make a day of it, with stalls and rides," said Winnie, her eyes sparkling at the possibility of a chance to stock up on astronomical goodies.

Valentine's eyes lit up. "Would there be a chance to do a little light haunting? Just for fun?"

"Oooh, YES!" cried Martin and Orlando, high-fiving each other.

Moon's eyes flicked from side to side, scanning the skyline, always vigilant. "But when?"

Winnie reached into her pocket and pulled out her trusty Star Diary. It told her exactly where the stars were supposed to be and when.

"Hang on," she said, thumbing through the well-worn pages. "Look!" she cried, pointing a finger. "A massive meteor shower called the

Northern Taurids is due, right over Starcross. A sky full of falling stars – what a show that will make! It's exactly what we need."

"Oooo!" crooned Orlando dreamily. "Lots and lots of glittery jewels, tumbly-tumbly out of the night. Twinkly, sparkly-shiny shooting stars."

"A meteor shower?" asked Knitbone. "How could an astonomer resist? When is it due?"

Winnie consulted her Star Diary. "Let me see, it's…ah. Oh dear." She looked up sheepishly. "In exactly seven days' time!"

"One week? Well there's no time to lose then!" gabbled Gabriel, pattering his feet and secretly thrilled at the opportunity to do some organizing.

"It'll need a name," said Valentine, taking a piece of paper and a stubby pencil out of Winnie's pocket, ready to make notes.

"How about Star Combat?" asked Martin, stabbing his sword at a tree.

"Ye Night of Light?" suggested Gabriel.

After a long, hard think, Orlando came up with "Shiny-Shiny-Shiny".

"I know, how about *The Night of a Billion Stars*?" barked Knitbone.

"Oh yes!" whinnied Moon. "That sounds very exciting. Rosabel would like that. But what about," she dropped her voice to a whisper, her eyes darting back and forth, "you-know-who?"

"Don't you worry about him," woofed Knitbone, carried away by his good idea and sounding more confident than he felt. "Galloping Jasper has no idea where you are. How is he going to find you? It would be like looking for a dog biscuit in a haystack. Or something like that anyway." He wagged his tail positively. "Just hide here until we can reunite you with Rosabel. Moon Starr – this is going to be the happy ending you've been waiting for!"

Chapter 7

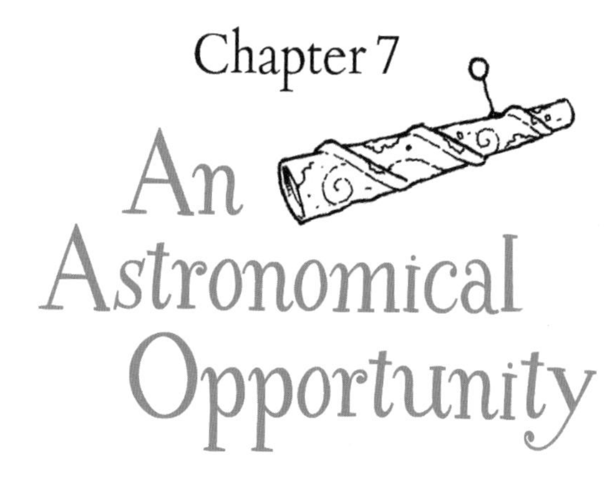

An Astronomical Opportunity

"And so you see," Winnie cheerily summed up, drawing her presentation to a close, "an astronomer's banquet would be the perfect autumn event to put on whilst the hat exhibition is closed. In the daytime we could have a fair – stalls, workshops, rides and talks – and at night we could hold the banquet in the conservatory by candlelight so everyone can see the falling stars through the glass ceiling."

"Yes, yes," said Lord Pepper, pondering

the idea, pacing up and down. "This is all rather exciting!"

"We'd need a guest speaker of course," said Winnie sweetly, pausing for a second before taking a deep breath. "What about the famous astronomer, Dr Rosabel Starr?"

Lord P pressed on, warming to the idea. "Well, you're the expert, Winnie, it's only right that you should choose. I don't know my astronomers from my astronauts. But a fair would be fun, don't you think?" he asked, looking at his wife. "It IS very quiet here without the visitors," he added wistfully.

Lady Pepper nodded her head. "I miss them all already. The old place is too quiet without the hustle and bustle. A meteor shower sounds like the ultimate light show…"

"And the stars here *are* very bright, now I come to think of it," interjected Lord Pepper. "No neighbours or street lamps for miles, not even a car to light up the lane. I remember my father saying to me that on a clear night, Starcross has the finest stars in England. Some of our Pepper ancestors were very interested in astronomy, I think. I'm not surprised though. Around here it's darker than a bat's armpit, eh, dear?" Lady Pepper laughed at his joke and spread acorn chutney on a cracker.

Suddenly Lord P frowned and folded his arms. "Just one thing bothers me though."

Uh-oh. Winnie held her breath. "Yes?"

"Will there be hats?"

Winnie let out a sigh of relief. "Yes, naturally. Of course! Why not? Astronaut helmets, pointy wizard hats with stars, top hats covered in moons – the sky's the limit!"

Lord Pepper clapped his hands, leaped for joy

and scampered off to his extensive hat collection to pick out some suitable examples. "Hooray for visitors!" he called behind him. "We Peppers have the best ideas, don't we, dear?"

"Hmmm? Oh yes, we certainly do." Lady Pepper had abandoned her buttercup cracker and was already pulling down piles of recipe books from the shelf. A banquet was something she could really get her teeth into. She even had an idea about the perfect cutlery for the event. She set to work on a space-themed menu, scribbling in her notebook and muttering away. "Black-Hole Gateau...Supernova Salad...Milky Way Mousse... Moon Cheese on Sticks..."

Now that the grown-ups were occupied, Winnie and the ghosts slipped away and got on with the important stuff. With only a week to plan, there was no time to lose.

Winnie sat at the computer, pulled up her sleeves and began to type.

To: drstarr@universityofthenorthpole.snow

From: pepperpopz@starnet.hat

Dear Dr Starr,

Please come to our astronomers' event – The Night of a Billion Stars – to celebrate the Northern Taurid meteor shower here at Starcross Hall on Saturday 29th October. We will be holding a space-themed banquet and would be over the moon if you would be our guest speaker.

There will be lots to eat, starry skies and some special surprises besides.

Please let us know as soon as possible.

Yours sincerely,

Winnie Pepper of Starcross Hall

She pressed *send* and turned to the others. "Now all we need is lots of stargazers."

They got on the phone and placed a full page advert in *The Astronomer's Weekly*:

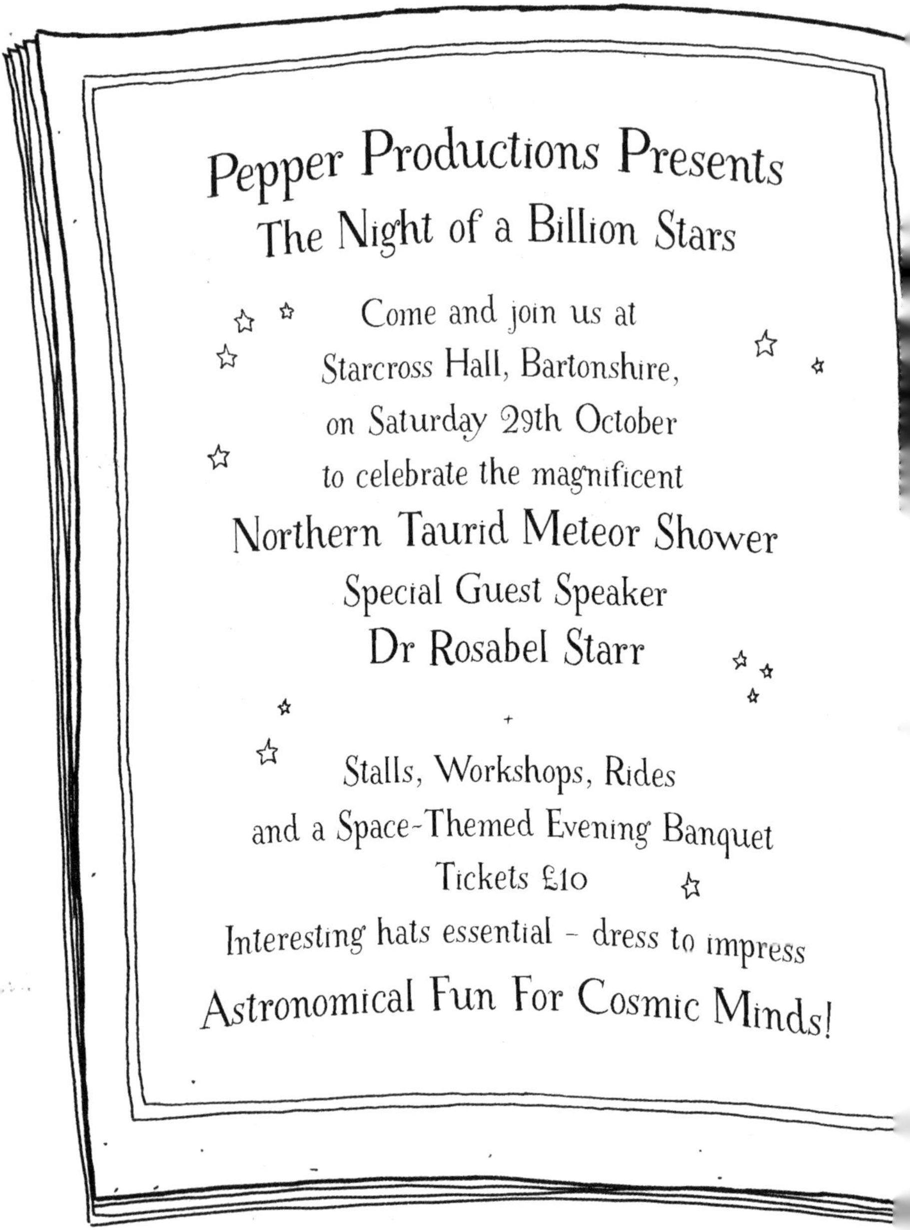

Pepper Productions Presents

The Night of a Billion Stars

Come and join us at
Starcross Hall, Bartonshire,
on Saturday 29th October
to celebrate the magnificent

Northern Taurid Meteor Shower

Special Guest Speaker

Dr Rosabel Starr

Stalls, Workshops, Rides
and a Space-Themed Evening Banquet
Tickets £10

Interesting hats essential – dress to impress

Astronomical Fun For Cosmic Minds!

Gabriel turned to Knitbone and whispered, “But what if Rosabel can’t come?”

“She has to,” woofed Knitbone. “There’s no other way.”

First thing the next morning, Winnie and the ghosts raced downstairs and turned on the computer. After what seemed like an age, a picture of a little envelope popped up.

YOU HAVE ONE NEW MESSAGE

"Open it! Open it!" barked Knitbone, bouncing around.

"Yes, open it, Winnie!" chorused the others,

crowding around her, looking over her shoulder.

Winnie stared at the screen for a moment and held her breath. *PLEASE let it be from Rosabel*, she thought, crossing her fingers hard. She clicked on the message…

Half a minute later, Winnie and the ghosts were racing across the courtyard. They skidded into the orchard, Winnie waving the printed out email in her outstretched hand.

"Moon! Moon! She wrote back!" Winnie stuck the email to the trunk of the apple tree with a drawing pin so that Moon could see for herself. She pointed at the sheet. "Look! ROSABEL IS COMING!"

The horse came very close and stared at the miraculous words, reading it over and over and over again, her big blue eyes skating over the words like ice. She gave a big toothy grin, her lip curling up, and with a joyful neigh, she read the email out loud.

Dear Winnie Pepper,

I was delighted to receive your invitation.

I've been very busy wrestling with The Great Bear (constellation Ursa Major), but fortunately have space in my diary. What a treat – an astronomer's banquet in such a remarkable location. I would be most honoured to come to Starcross. What astronomer wouldn't?

I hope your stargazers will enjoy my new lecture, entitled "Juggling the Rings of Saturn."

I'll be there at 6 p.m.

Kushti Bok!

Dr Rosabel Starr

"What does 'Kushti Bok' mean?" asked Martin, standing on tiptoe to see the reply.

"It's Romany for 'good luck'. You see? That proves it! She's still the same old Rosabel!" Skittish with energy, Moon was almost popping with excitement. "Oh my goodness!" she sang, shaking her mane and jingling her bells. "It's real! *Really* real! I KNEW she wouldn't let us down." Moon flicked her ears, flared her nostrils and did a little tap dance: *clippity-clop, clippity-clop!* "Rosabel's coming home!" she sang.

"Yes, about that," said Knitbone doubtfully, eyeing the wagon's shabby curtains and cracked windows. "It looks like you could do with a bit of help on that front."

Moon looked at the caravan and sagged a little. "Ah yes. I suppose it could do with a bit of a spring clean."

"A spring clean?" honked Gabriel, pecking at the peeling paint. "What it needs is an autumn overhaul!" He kicked a wheel and a spindle fell off. "Oh dear, this won't do at all," he warbled bossily.

"We can't have Rosabel seeing the caravan like this, can we? It needs to be shipshape and smart. You need to look your best, Moon. Spirits of Starcross," barked Knitbone, wagging his tail, "follow me. We've got work to do!"

Five minutes later, Winnie and the ghosts were heaving a wheelbarrow full of pots of paint, fabric, panes of glass, hammers, drills and glue over to the orchard.

Moon fluttered her long eyelashes and nodded her head bashfully. "Roojoo was right. You really are wonderful. Thank you, my Beloved friends."

Full of hope, love and mouthfuls of ginger biscuits, S.O.S. set about the daunting task of returning the caravan to its former glory. They fixed the shafts, mended the wheels, replaced the windows and painted the whole wagon the rich, deep, dark blue of a midnight sky. They went over the lettering *Moon and the Starrs* so it was clear and bright and as good as new.

Checking in her book, Winnie realized that the caravan had been painted with animal constellations: The Great Bear, the Dog Star, Leo the lion and Cygnus the swan.

On the very front was Pegasus the horse.

With a steady paw, Valentine carefully retouched all of the fading stars in shining silver so the constellations twinkled once more.

By the end of the day, the wagon's lamps glinted and the freshly painted stars shone brightly. Inside the caravan, the feather bed was plumped up like a snowy cloud and the floor was polished until it gleamed.

Orlando re-blacked the little stove and fresh kindling wood was put inside, ready for Rosabel to make a cup of tea. The wagon was a true beauty. They all stood back and looked at their handiwork. Knitbone gave a big yawn. "Pawfection!"

That night they all sat around the campfire, tired but happy. "It's lucky we're so good at housework really," said Valentine, rubbing dirt from his nose.

"Thank you so much," said Moon, admiring the transformation. She gave her tail a joyful swish and jerked her head up. "Rosabel is coming and the wagon looks as good as new." She did another little tap dance and jingled merrily. "I feel on top of the world."

"Eez tip-top to see you all cheered up, lady pony," said Orlando, clapping his tiny hands.

"If you don't mind me asking, Moon," enquired Knitbone, nibbling away at a ginger biscuit, "how *did* you come to lose your special person?"

At the memory, Moon hung her head, her moist eyes shining in the firelight. Eventually she began. "The Starrs were a very old travelling family, fond of tradition. My grandmother pulled this caravan first of all. Her name was Eclipse, because she was black as night. It used to be her name on the sign. Then it was my mother's – she was called Comet because she was so fast. Then I was born and eventually the sign bore my name."

"You're home-grown like me!" woofed Knitbone, looking across at Winnie.

"Yes. I was with the family all my life and – oh! – what a happy life it was," said Moon, cheering up at the memory. "In those days this caravan was overflowing with Starrs. We were a colourful bunch! You can fit quite a lot of people in a caravan when you try. There was Pa Starr, Ma Starr, Beshli, Ruben, Dika, Kizzy,

Nadia, Marko and Tomas. Then the last Starr was born – beautiful baby Rosabel – and she was the apple of my eye. We became firm friends straight away. Even as a little tot she used to sit on my back and fall asleep, her little hands lost in my mane as I jingled along. We were all very content as the years went by, living our simple family life on the road."

Moon shook her head and her bridle tinkled. "But all that was a very long time ago. Old Ma and Pa died, the brothers and sisters grew up and moved into their own caravans to raise their own families. All except for Rosabel, whose dreams lay in following the stars. Starr by name and starry-eyed by nature. We were a team, going everywhere together, as she recorded the changes in the night sky, looking for interesting signs, painting constellations on the wagon as we went. Her favourite was Pegasus, the winged horse."

Winnie looked up into the darkness. She could see the constellation in the night sky, a twinkling pattern of stars sparkling above their heads.

Moon continued. "Rosabel and I were hardly ever apart, except for the times she went to fetch food or firewood. A Moon and a Starr – she always said that we were a friendship made in Heaven."

"Every pan needs a lid, every sock needs a shoe," nodded Gabriel quietly, remembering his own special person. "Everybody needs a special somebody." His heart remained devoted to Winstanley Pepper, the absent-minded Starcross scholar, who had hatched Gabriel out of an egg over 350 years ago.

Moon gave a deep, long sigh. "One night we stopped at a village. We normally kept to the back lanes, away from the lights and the crowds, but I had a loose shoe that needed fixing and

Rosabel worried about me going lame." Everyone listened closely as Moon's voice dropped to something only just above a whisper.

"As we pulled into the village square late that summer evening, everybody stopped to admire the painted wagon. People kept saying I must be a lucky horse – they were very complimentary about my blue eyes and long, white mane. Soon a horse dealer began to pester Rosabel with a fistful of money. But Rosabel just laughed and waved him away. She kissed me on the forelock, tethered me to a tree and went to find a blacksmith." Moon dropped her head and shut her eyes. "I never saw her again."

"What? But..." asked Winnie, shocked. "But why?"

"I was stolen by the horse dealer the minute Rosabel turned her back. He hid me far away, chained up in the middle of a forest. I waited and I waited but Rosabel never found me.

Without her, there was no reason to go on. I died of a broken heart."

A tear rolled down her long velvety nose. She gave a big sniff. "Of course, then the horse dealer said the wagon was cursed and left it to rot amongst the trees. But little did anyone know my spirit was still tied to it."

"Bound to the home, the place where our happiest memories lie," whispered Knitbone, looking at the others. "We understand."

"It took me a while to understand that I was

a ghost. In fact, it wasn't until Galloping Jasper moved into the caravan that I understood that I must have died. He said that I was his horse and that my new name was to be Black Bertha, not Moon Starr any more." Moon shook her white mane, her bells jangling, and gave a defiant snort. "But secretly I've never stopped looking for Rosabel."

She raised her head to the skies once more and gazed at Pegasus. "For years I've been looking up at the constellations, hoping that Rosabel is watching the same stars."

The other Beloveds sat dumbstruck, not knowing what to say. How terrible and awful and sad. How brave she was.

Poor Moon.

Poor Rosabel.

Chapter 9
Chop-chop

Every morning that week the Beloveds worked like fury to make sure everything was in place for The Night of a Billion Stars. Gabriel made a long list of jobs and ticked them off one by one whilst Winnie made the necessary phone calls. Martin kept Moon's supplies of ginger biscuits topped up and Valentine made some very beautiful signs using paint and glitter from Winnie's art box.

One morning, Lady Pepper levered up a

floorboard in the kitchen with a crowbar, lifting out a dusty box of antique silverware. Inside, lying in their faded blue velvet nest, were dozens of beautiful medieval spoons.

She had hidden them long ago, on the advice of relatives, as spoons had a peculiar way of disappearing at Starcross. Each one had the name of a different constellation engraved on it in swirly writing, the letters "AP" stamped on the handle.

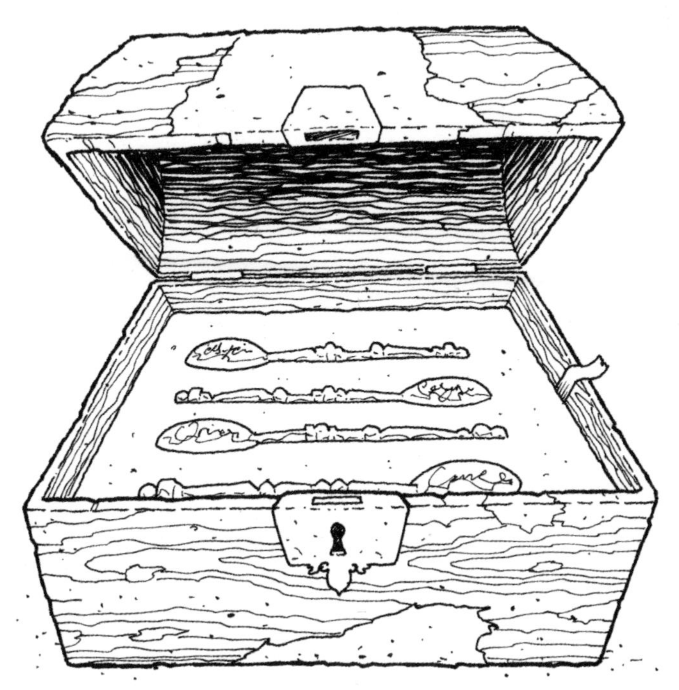

"They're amazing," breathed Winnie in wonder, looking over her mother's shoulder. "What does AP stand for?"

"Not sure, dear, maybe a long-lost ancestor," said Lady Pepper. "But they are ideal, don't you think? I thought about them as soon as you suggested an astronomer's banquet. Just had to remember where I'd stashed them."

Orlando was instantly besotted. He had never seen such bewitching items and fell head over tail in love with them on the spot.

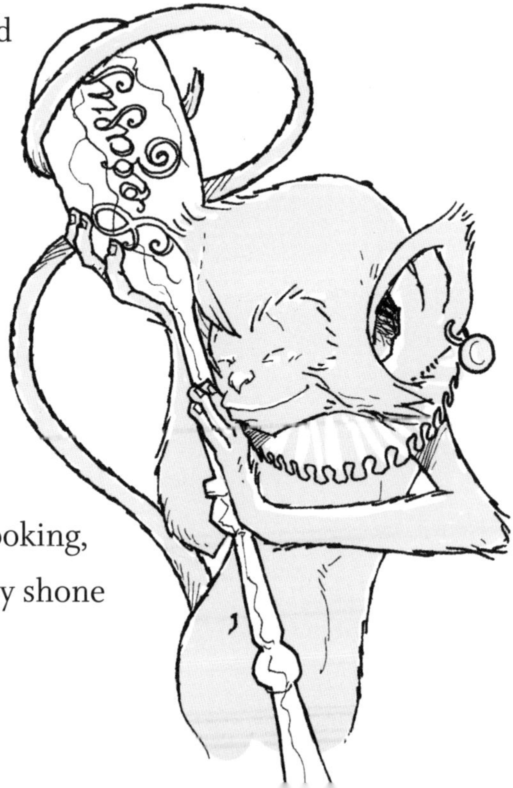

When Lady Pepper wasn't looking, the little monkey shone

them adoringly, one by one, crooning a lullaby and telling them stories. Then, when they sparkled like supernovas, he lowered them gently back in their special velvety box, like babies back in their cradles.

Whilst Orlando's mornings were busy with spoon-bliss, the others got on with sorting out the old conservatory. Throughout the rest of the week, Winnie and Knitbone yanked down thick, green ropes of tangled ivy and vines that had been growing there for as long as anyone could remember. The ghosts chopped and Winnie hacked and sawed. Martin rubbed the grime from the windows and the conservatory seemed to heave a sigh of relief as the low autumn light gushed in. Knitbone and Valentine used their powerful legs to fill up their "archaeology holes" with soil and then covered them with stray tiles until it all looked pancake-flat.

Gabriel then got to work, sliding about on

his bottom, polishing the black and white chequerboard floor to ice-rink standards. Rats and bats were shooed away and the fountain was emptied of shoes, hats and interesting books. Winnie dragged in ancient tables and chairs and laid them out in long lines. Slowly the conservatory began to look like a glassy wonderland.

After working so hard in the mornings they gave themselves the afternoons off, as it meant they could spend time with their new friend. Getting to know Moon Starr was like opening a room and discovering that inside it brimmed with mysterious treasures.

Moon knew lots of things. She taught them how to make hedgerow medicines out of blackberries and cobwebs. As if by magic, she could always find bubbling springs of sparkling, fresh water and she knew exciting words, like "hotchi-witchi" for hedgehog and "potchi" for pocket. She taught them how to spark an instant campfire on a rainy day and how to tell when the wind was about to change its mind.

On Friday afternoon, the last day before the banquet, Moon taught them a special secret, her blue eyes twinkling.

"Dearest friends, because of you, tomorrow I will see Rosabel again. This will be my dream come true." Moon looked very solemn. "Kindness is something travelling folk never forget and I would like to repay you in some way." Moon jingled her bells and her harness glinted in the low autumn light. "I'm going to share a secret with you, one that has been passed down from Romany to Romany for hundreds of years." The ghosts sat up straight and listened closely.

"We have a special travelling language which no one else knows: the Patteran. It's a secret way of leaving messages along the road to let your friends know where you have gone," explained Moon.

"How do you mean?" asked Knitbone, scratching his ear. He knew that dogs left special messages on lamp posts but also felt that maybe now wasn't the right moment to bring it up.

"A series of clues. A snapped twig here, a clump of mud there...to a house dweller it would look like nothing."

"Like a message written in invisible ink?" asked Gabriel.

"Yes," whinnied Moon, "only with leaves. It's amazing what people don't see, even when it's under their very noses. You wouldn't spot it if you didn't know what to look for. But to a Romany, they are like signposts. Sometimes we have to move on quickly, maybe in the middle of the night, particularly if there is danger. It's a foolproof way of finding each other again, sometimes over hundreds of miles. It's a very useful skill. Here, I'll show you…" She picked leaves from the hedgerows with her teeth and bent twigs with her hoof. "This means 'gone right'," she said, laying down the twig. "And this means 'we turned around'," she said, placing a small bunch of leaves in a pile. "Now you try."

They spent a fun afternoon playing hide and seek, tracking each other around the Estate.

Learning the Patteran was like being able to speak a secret language that only a chosen few knew. It felt special and the hours flew by. Finally, when it got too dark to see anything any more, they trooped off to bed, waving goodnight to their fascinating friend.

"Goodnight, pretty pony-lady," crooned Orlando.

"Sweet dreams, fair maiden," chimed Valentine and Gabriel, sending Winnie into fits of giggles.

Martin held his sword triumphantly in the air. "Just one more sleep to go until Rosabel! Hoorah and hoozah!"

"Goodnight, Moon!" called Knitbone. "Sleep tight. Tomorrow is your special day. Time to get some beauty sleep!"

"We'll be busy all day with the astronomers tomorrow," said Winnie, patting Moon's neck. "But we'll come and get you in the evening. Will you be alright here until then?"

"Alright, Winnie Pepper? I should say so." Moon let out a huge, happy, horsey yawn and settled down to sleep under the apple tree. "Tomorrow Rosabel and I will be together again. I've never felt more alive…"

Exhausted by a week of work and play, the ghosts and Winnie trooped back across the moonlit courtyard, climbed the stairs, clambered into bed and went out like a row of birthday candles.

Chapter 10

Space Tourists

Next morning, the Peppers were up bright and early, sorting out the final details of the day. The Night of a Billion Stars had finally arrived.

Lord Pepper had been up with the lark, still agonizing over which outfit to wear. Finally settling on his trusty wizard costume, he sprinkled silver star confetti across the tablecloths, laid out the sparkling cutlery and glasses and spent the next few hours making hats out of the paper napkins. From the deafening sounds of clattering and banging that were coming from the kitchen, it seemed that his wife was also in full swing.

Since dawn, Lady Pepper had been slaving over a hot stove, feverishly creating weird and wonderful delights for the evening ahead. Pots bubbled and pans sizzled as she stood, deep in concentration over her space-themed creations. Unusually for her, she had only set fire to the kitchen once. Ever positive, she merely saw it as a learning experience, noting in her diary for future reference that rocket fuel was *not* suitable for crisping meringues, no matter how much of a good idea it may seem at the time.

In honour of the evening ahead, Lady Pepper had already renamed her workspace The Kosmic Kitchen, and was wearing a full astronaut suit, complete with glass helmet and breathing apparatus. Winnie and Knitbone entered the room cautiously.

"Isn't it a bit early for fancy dress?" asked Winnie, eyeing her mother's oxygen tanks.

"Pardon? What was that, Winnie? Sorry, can't hear you, dear!" Lady Pepper's voice sounded very muffled. "I'm wearing a spacesuit! Stops me crying over the onions! Can't chat, very busy, chop-chop!"

Knitbone rested his chin on the edge of the kitchen table, which was groaning under the weight of plates and ingredients. From here he could see, lying in a puddle of pink sauce, a list of dishes scribbled on the back of an old envelope. He reached over, picked it up and trotted across the courtyard to the caravan. Inside was Valentine, waiting patiently with his colouring pencils.

"Here's what's cooking in Lady P's crazy kitchen," woofed Knitbone cheerfully, placing the soggy offering on the front steps. "Time to work your arty magic."

Valentine picked the drippy list up with obvious distaste and then disappeared inside. He reappeared an hour later with an armful of smart new menus for the tables, covered in swoops and flourishes, with drawings of planets in the corners and even more glitter on the edges.

Pepper Productions
in association with
The Kosmic Kitchen
presents

A Night of a Billion Stars
Astronomers' Banquet

☆ Starters ☆

Solar sausages and moon cheese on sticks
Starship soup

☆ Mains ☆

Quantum quiche
Particle accelerator pie with gravity gravy
Red dwarf risotto
Galileo eggs (sunny side up)
Diet option: Sat-a-lite salad

☆ Puddings ☆

Intergalactic ice-cream with astro jelly
Rings of Saturn doughnuts with cosmic custard
followed by kosmic koffee and moon macaroons

The Beloveds trotted back over to the conservatory and placed the menus neatly on the white tablecloths amongst the sparkling spoons and star-spangled confetti. Everything looked, as Lord Pepper would say, simply smashing.

A loud tooting came from the courtyard and the ghosts went to investigate. A big lorry had arrived, its engine running. The cab window rolled down and a big bald man with a tattoo of a comet on his head leaned out. "Delivery for the Starcross Estate. Who's in charge?"

"I am," said Winnie, standing tall. "Space carousel over there, please," she pointed, "and the Moon Buggy rides can go over there. Please leave a space for the orchestra, they have a lot of instruments." She sounded terribly grown-up and Knitbone stood very close to her, quite overcome with pride. Everything was coming together, just like they planned.

By noon a long queue of traffic was waiting outside the gates and the air was electric with anticipation. Visitors were leaning out of their windows, revving their engines and honking their horns. There were vans with satellite dishes on top, rocket-shaped motorbikes with aerials

and a monster truck covered in flying saucers. There was even a double-decker bus with a big telescope on its roof. Winnie was thrilled; she couldn't wait to meet all the astronomers. The ghosts were full of beans too.

"*Will* we be able to do a bit of haunting, Winnie?" asked Martin, munching a big chunk out of a ginger biscuit.

"Oh, yes!" woofed Knitbone, panting enthusiastically. "Can we, Winnie? Just a bit of light spooking, for old times' sake?"

Winnie thought for a moment. "Well, I don't see why not. Starcross is known for its ghosts, even if Mum and Dad still think I'm making you all up. Just be your normal, spooky selves and keep the haunting friendly."

Orlando reached for a pink wafer and opened his mouth, only to have it whipped away at the last minute.

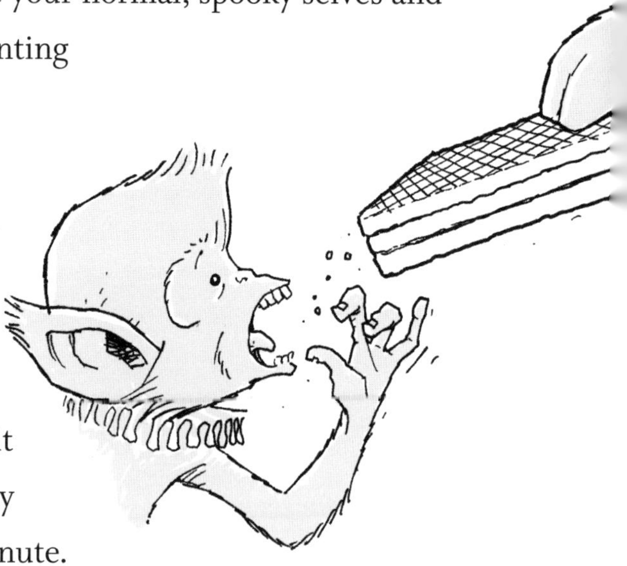

"No!" said Valentine. "You heard Winnie. Today we are on our best behaviour: ginger biscuits only. Strictly no naughty biscuits."

Winnie flipped open Bertie's pocket watch. At last, the moment had come. "It's time!" she announced.

"Well done, everybody!" said Knitbone.

Together they counted down the last few seconds. "Five…four…three…two…one!" With a flourish Winnie threw open the gates. "Welcome to Starcross!" she cried to the cheering crowds. "Welcome to The Night of a Billion Stars!"

Chapter 11

Divide and Fool

The stargazers arriving at Starcross were fascinating. Some astronomers had heads as bald as eggs and some had long, long beards, woven into plaits. One sensibly dressed lady in pearls and half-moon spectacles looked like she might be a teacher, until she revealed her name to be Jupiter Astrogirl. There was a man dressed as a rocket and another dressed as an alien.

Lord Pepper had been given the job of greeting everyone at the information desk.

"Wow!" said the rocket man, looking up at the house looming over them. "Starcross Hall is out of this world!"

"No, no, my dear fellow," explained Lord P patiently, adjusting his wizard's hat. "I can assure you that you are still very much on planet Earth." He patted the man affectionately on his pointy rocket head, adding, "Are you a beginner astronomer?"

The man looked confused as Lord Pepper gently ushered him along. He chuckled to himself. Earlier on, one of the stargazers had even asked if "the famous Starcross Spooks" would be making an appearance. These space folk were indeed bonkers.

Standing in the middle of the teeming, smiling crowds, Winnie and the ghosts looked around them, drinking in their surroundings. The orchestra began to play loud classical pieces from *The Planets* by Holst, filling the air with celestial drama as moon buggies vroomed around the Estate, complete with satellite dishes and NASA flags.

Traders sold telescopes, books, lenses, films and various assorted items, like mugs with pictures of planets on them and giant marbles with galaxies inside. There were T-shirts that said *Heavens Above* and vacuum-packed freeze-dried space snacks. Queues formed for lectures entitled "Do You Believe In Aliens?" and "Dark Matters – Why?" They even had a drive-in cinema showing films of the first moon landings. Starcross was buzzing once more.

"Oooh, it looks brilliant! I think everyone's arrived. Can we start haunting now?" asked Martin, jumping up and down. "Can we? Can we?"

"Definitely," grinned Winnie, who had her eye on a beautiful poster of the solar system for her bedroom and wanted to buy one before they sold out. "Rosabel won't be here until this evening and Moon is safely tucked away in the orchard, so we can relax until then. Go and have some fun! You all deserve it."

As the Beloveds romped away, Winnie saw people jump and giggle, gently tickled by invisible paws. She felt a warm glow of pride; the ghosts were such professionals.

Winnie was having a cracking afternoon. She'd bought her space poster, and was now chatting to astronomers, discussing the space–time continuum and slurping a space slushie.

Lord Pepper mingled with the guests, admiring their scale models of solar systems and cooing over the size of their telescopes. He'd already swapped his wizard hat for an intergalactic alien costume and was charging around the grounds with a cosmic ray blaster, going "*ZAP-ZAZ-ZAZ-ZAP*", much to the delight of the astronomers.

"Nice outfit, Dad!" laughed Winnie as they passed each other in the crowd.

"Thanks! Got my vest on underneath, though," he said, absent-mindedly zapping a toddler dressed in a spacesuit. "Jolly chilly in the house today for some reason, weasels must have been at the electrics again. Nothing like a bit of running about to warm you up!"

Winnie's mother came wandering out of the house, a scarf and bobble hat clearly visible through her glass helmet. She was shivering, muttering to herself and pulling up stray carrots growing in the hedge. "House is going haywire,"

she complained. "Doors slamming, lights going on and off, towers of plates slipping off the kitchen table – *CRASH-SMASH-BANG!* Hardly got any crockery left. And now – today of all days – the box of antique star spoons has disappeared!" She bumbled back inside, arms full of muddy root vegetables, grumbling to herself.

Smashing plates? Missing star spoons? Oh no. This was really *very* naughty, even by monkey standards. She decided to put it down to high spirits and crossed her fingers it was just a one-off.

Winnie was working on a plan to get the spoons back when a cross-looking mother marched out of the face-painting tent, a chain of children in tow. "I asked for lovely colourful pictures of Venus, Jupiter and Mars," she scowled. Instead each child had the words GHOSTS ROOL painted on their foreheads in smudgy black crayon.

Winnie was shocked: this was *not* friendly haunting. She knew the Beloveds missed spooking but this was downright rude. Inside the tent the face-painter looked very confused, staring at the black crayon in his hands, not really understanding what had just happened.

Winnie was about to go and find the ghosts in order to deliver some stern words, when suddenly loud screams came from outside, filling the air with terror.

"What *now*?" Winnie cried, as she squeezed back through the crowds again and hurtled towards the noise, her plaits flying in the wind.

A deafening racket was coming from the space carousel. Normally quite sedate, the ride was spinning wildly out of control. It whizzed

and whirled, round and round, as the riders shrieked, desperately clinging onto the poles of their space-pigs and moon-cows.

People's screams rose higher and higher over the jangly music, a speeded-up tune which sounded as if it had been composed by hysterical chipmunks.

Winnie ran around the back and quickly inspected the controls. Someone had turned the dial up to WARP-SPEED. She yanked the plug out of its power socket and slowly, slowly, the carousel came to its senses. Terrified people slid off their star-unicorns, hanging off the horns, clambering, staggering and stumbling in dizzy circles.

"Right. WHAT is going on?" hissed Winnie, hands on hips, spotting Knitbone watching horrified from the sidelines. "SOMEBODY has been at the naughty pink wafers. This is definitely not light spooking. What do you lot think you're up to?"

"ME?" Knitbone looked wide-eyed and innocent. "It's not me! Maybe it's Valentine – he likes things to go fast."

Hearing his name, Valentine bounded over. "Me?" he snorted, whiskers quivering in outrage. "I am the Beloved of a noble knight!"

Winnie scanned the crowd, only to be greeted by the sight of lots of fake black eyes. "What on earth…?" said Winnie. She had noticed a telescope with a sign hanging off it that said *LOOK*. She inspected the eyepiece to find it was covered in black soot. She held up an accusing black finger. "Is this someone's idea of a joke? Is this Martin's doing?" she asked crossly.

"No, it most certainly is not!" exclaimed a small indignant voice from behind her. "What about Orlando? He's crazier than a coconut. Or maybe it's Gabriel!"

"How dare you!" Gabriel marched over and fixed the little hamster with his hardest glare. "I am a *librarian* goose! How could you suggest such a thing?"

"Now, now, everybody, calm down," said Knitbone. "There must be some logical explanation."

"Yes," honked Gabriel. "The explanation is that you don't trust me!"

"Or me!" piped up Martin.

"Or me!" scowled Valentine, folding his arms. "I thought friends were supposed to trust each other."

"No! I mean, yes!" protested Winnie. "Well of

course we do… It's just that…" But it was too late. The Beloveds had stormed off in an almighty huff, on the warpath to find Orlando.

"Oh dear." Winnie's good mood evaporated like morning mist. This wasn't at all what she had in mind. They were supposed to be having a happy time and now everything was going wrong.

"Don't worry, Winnie," whimpered Knitbone, his tail between his legs. "It's just a hiccup; they'll be back. A few ginger biscuits and soon everyone will be friends again, you'll see."

"This looks like monkey madness," said Winnie with a heavy sigh. Everybody knew that after a few pink wafers, Orlando was unstoppable.

Knitbone hated Winnie being sad; it made him feel rainy inside. He noticed a battered old van parked to the side of the carousel. It had planets and the word "Astrology" painted on it in big letters. Sitting in the doorway was an old woman, offering to read people's palms. Gold earrings dangled from her ears and she wore a floral scarf on her head. A little chalkboard leaned against the van, saying *Your future is brighter than the stars.*

"Look, Winnie," woofed Knitbone, hoping it might cheer her up. "A fortune teller! There's not even a queue!"

Winnie gave a shrug. Why not? After the afternoon she'd had, she could do with a bit of light-hearted nonsense.

"Hello," said Winnie to the old woman, placing some coins on the table. "Can you read my palm and tell me that everything is going to be alright, please? Only, I'm having a bit of a bad day."

The old lady took Winnie's upturned palm and inspected it, screwing up her eyes and wiggling her eyebrows.

"You have an extraordinarily long lifeline, young lady. Quite remarkable. You have made special friends…unusual friends…" Her eyebrows suddenly shot up.

"What is it?" asked Winnie.

"You have a visitor," muttered the old lady, scrutinizing Winnie's palm.

Knitbone nudged Winnie's leg. "She must mean Moon," whispered Knitbone in surprise. "This lady's better than I'd expected."

"Yes, that's right," said Winnie to the old lady. "Another special friend. A white horse, maybe?"

"No. Not a white horse. Not a friend neither." The old lady's face drained of colour and she dropped Winnie's hand like a stone. "Er…" she stammered. "I have to go now. Goodbye." With this she speedily bundled everything into the van, slammed the door and screeched off out of the gates.

"But what about the banquet? What about the meteor shower?" Winnie raced after her, leaving Knitbone behind, running up the dusky lane. "And what do you mean," she shouted after the retreating van, "'not a friend'?"

Knitbone's tail drooped and he sat down. Today was not turning out to be their lucky day after all.

"All going swimmingly, is it?"

A distinctive, screechy, sarcastic voice came from inside the big hedge. "Everything hunky-dory?"

Brilliant, thought Knitbone gloomily. *Mrs Jones. Just what I need.*

A grey, spindly spider sidled out of the branches, watching Knitbone with her glittery eyes. She blew him a vinegary kiss.

"What do YOU want?"

"Tut tut. Now why would I want anything from you, Knickerface Pickle?"

"Because you are a Bad Egg, Mrs Jones, and you are always making trouble." Knitbone gave an impatient sigh.

"You're making proper spectacles of yourselves over that shaggy old dobbin and her wonky wheelie bin, you know. She's not welcome here. Trespasser she is, even worser than that nasty tiger and his stupid tent." Mrs Jones cackled and scuttled back into the hedge. "Not for long though, not for long."

"No, not for long!" barked Knitbone angrily. "Because Rosabel will be here very soon and they'll be reunited, so what do you think of that? Ha!"

But as Mrs Jones retreated away into the darkness, Knitbone had a niggling feeling. His hackles twitched and his nose itched. His instincts told him something was definitely not right.

Knitbone looked up into the darkening sky. A sparkling net of stars had already fallen over Starcross. There was no time to think any more about it. Rosabel was due to arrive any moment.

Chapter 12

A Beast of a Machine

Gabriel, Valentine and Martin stood fidgeting in the hallway, still in a bit of a huff. Orlando had reappeared and was forced to protest his innocence most strongly. Nobody believed him so he pulled an egg-cosy over his head and faced the wall in a massive sulk. Knitbone leaned against Winnie's leg in a show of loyalty and tried to be positive. Not everything had gone to plan, but the grand finale was approaching and, after all, this was about Moon, not them. The astronomers were already in the conservatory, nibbling at Lady Pepper's Moon Cheese on Sticks, waiting excitedly for the arrival of the special guest speaker and renowned expert on the night sky, Dr Rosabel Starr.

Nibbling her nails, Winnie looked at the clock in the hallway. It said ten past six. Rosabel was late. Where was she? Knitbone hoped and prayed that she hadn't changed her mind. Through the open doorway he eyed the sky: no sign of a meteor shower yet either. They shuffled and fidgeted in the open doorway, looking up the road for any sound of a car.

Suddenly Knitbone's ears shot up. He could hear the faintest rumbling in the distance, but it wasn't the noise of a car engine. Quickly the noise rose to a grumble, then a clatter, then a clamour and then the night sky filled with a thunderous *whop-whop-whop*, like the sound of a thousand wonky washing machines on spin cycle.

A bright beam of light sliced the night in two and swept across the courtyard, up and over the crumbling towers of the house and back down again.

"What on earth—?" Winnie stood up and squinted up into the bright light. "Oh my heavens… Knitbone, is that HER?" she shouted, her plaits whipping wildly about in the wind. She jumped up and down, clapping her hands. "WOWZERS! SHE'S GOT A HELICOPTER!"

The huge machine hovered for a moment, like an enormous roaring dragonfly, glossy midnight blue and covered in silver stars. As it settled in the courtyard it blew the last of the leaves from the trees, sending them tumbling in all directions.

It's just like a modern version of the caravan, thought Knitbone, as the Beloveds forgot that they were supposed to be sulking and instead started high-fiving and whooping. "Woohoo! Rosabel's here! The Starr from afar has landed!"

Lord and Lady Pepper crossed the courtyard, now dressed in their banquet finery, to greet their guest of honour. As the helicopter hurricane faded to a light gale, the curved glass door popped open and out stepped an elderly lady. She was wrapped up warmly in white furs

and was wearing flying goggles, her lecture notes tucked firmly under her arm. Rosabel looked surprisingly sprightly for a ninety-six-year-old. She lifted up her goggles and pushed them back into her white hair, her kind, dark eyes creased into smiles.

Knitbone couldn't help wandering over for a curious sniff: Rosabel Starr smelled very strongly of adventure.

"Ah! The Peppers of Starcross Hall! What an honour to finally meet you! So sorry I'm late, had to stop over to refuel. That's the problem with choppers. They're always hungry." She reached out a glove to shake hands. "I can't stay very long as I have to be in Portugal by morning. It's something of a flying visit, I'm afraid. I have something for you here." She reached into the helicopter. "A small token of my appreciation…"

But before she could finish her sentence, Lord Pepper interrupted her. "Dr Starr, what a pleasure," he said, adjusting the ray blaster on his belt. "We are so pleased you could spare the time. And what a fine vehicle! I must say you certainly travel in style. This is our daughter Winnie; say hello, Winnie."

Winnie stepped forward and held out her hand. "Hello, Dr Starr!" said Winnie with a big sigh of relief. "You have no idea how pleased we are to see you."

Rosabel Starr stopped in her tracks, poleaxed by the sight of the girl who stood before her. For quite a while she peered and stared so hard that Winnie thought she might have ginger biscuit crumbs in her hair.

"Winnie, you say?" she asked, shaking Winnie's outstretched hand slowly. "You are Winifred Pepper? Are you absolutely sure?"

"Yes, she certainly is," trilled Lord Pepper, butting in and keen to hurry everything along. "Lady Winifred Clementina Violet Araminta Pepper at your service. Although she's just wonderful Winnie to us, of course! This way, please! No time to lose! Chop-chop."

Before Dr Starr could ask any more questions, Lord Pepper whisked her towards the conservatory, steering her by the elbow. He placed a mortar board wrapped in tinfoil on her head with a wink. "Here, pop this on, there's a dear. Only a hat makes you look more, you know," he patted her shoulder, "*professional.*"

"But, Dad," called Winnie, looking frustrated, "I need a word with Dr Starr—"

"I know you're a fan, Winnie, but your space questions will have to wait until later," he called back. "We've got enough food to fill up a black hole and one hundred and forty-three astronomers very keen to hear what Dr Starr has to say."

"*Daddy, it's important!*" Winnie called after them. But they had already disappeared around the corner. Suddenly a loud cheer rose from the conservatory as the astronomers broke into applause, overjoyed at the arrival of their guest of honour.

"Don't worry, Winnie," woofed Knitbone, bouncing about, feeling a lot happier about everything. "It's probably for the best. Rosabel's in for a bit of a shock, remember. We'll be sure to catch her as soon as she comes out." He wagged his tail, stood up on his back legs and did a little pirouette of joy. "At last! The time has come to tell Moon the good news; that her person is here safe and sound!"

Eager to see Moon again, they all bounded happily over to the orchard.

"Moon! Moon!" called Winnie, shining her

torch through the trees. "You won't believe it, she's here! Rosabel is actually *here* at Starcross!"

But beneath the boughs of the apple tree, where the wagon should have been, there was nothing but a grassy space: green, frosty – and completely empty.

Chapter 13

Lost Soul

"Moon!" honked Gabriel, spinning around on his feet, looking about for the caravan as Martin searched behind the tree. "Moon!" he called. "Moon, where are you?"

"Where is she?" panicked Valentine, looking about and whipping his ears back and forth. Orlando inspected the grass. Aside from the dents in the ground where the wheels had been, there was no trace that the wagon had been there at all.

“Oh no, oh no, OH NO!” wailed Knitbone. “Moon!” he barked, looking anxiously about. A terribly bad feeling washed over him as his tail crept between his legs. “MOON!” He began to howl at the sky. “MOOOOOOOOON!”

A bitter little snigger came from above. “So, the horse has bolted!” Mrs Jones shot out of the apple tree, sliding down a woolly thread like a fireman down a pole. She spun gleefully, just out of reach.

Knitbone glared up at her. "YOU!" He bared his teeth and snarled. "Where is she, you…you… creep?"

"Tee-hee!" Mrs Jones zipped back up her thread like an evil yo-yo. "Told you she'd be gone soon, didn't I? Back where she belongs. Shame, you only just missed her. 'Fraid she didn't have time to say goodbye. That Galloping Jasper's ever so handsome – scars and everything." She swooned slightly. "When a gentleman asks for help, how can a lady refuse?"

The ghosts gaped in horror. Winnie watched in shock as all of the pieces fell into place. Of course. All of those nasty haunting tricks weren't the Beloveds' style at all. Orlando might be naughty, but his heart was in the right place. The cold house, the flickering lights, the smashing plates, frightening people, showing off…all typical human ghost behaviour. Jasper must have been there all day, right under their noses, sneaking around the grounds of Starcross. Even the fortune teller had known. A hot flush of shame rose up from her feet.

Orlando was pop-eyed with anxiety. "*GALLOPING JASPER!* The bad-man ghost? Oh noes-oh, noes-oh, noes!"

"HUMAN ghosts?" Knitbone's eyes were huge with disbelief. "I knew you were bad, Mrs Jones, but I didn't thing you were *mad*. You've gone too far this time."

Suddenly Gabriel became white-hot with rage. For such a bookish bird, he had quite a temper when crossed. He flapped his wings and flew up into the tree, grabbing Mrs Jones in his beak.

"Gerroff, you oversized chicken!" she shrieked.

"Not until you tell us where Jasper and Moon are! How on earth did he find her?" Knitbone snarled. "Where is she?"

"Tracked her on foot, didn't he? Cunning as a fox with a calculator, he is! And now you're too late! They're on their way back to London again, where all the proper action is, not like this boring dump. YOU'LL NOT *NEVER EVER* SEE HER AGAIN, SO *HA*! Hoorah, hoozah and ya boo sucks to you. Soppy, happy endings are sick-making anyway."

Gabriel spat out Mrs Jones in disgust. Sitting on the frosty grass, Mrs Jones clacked her fangs and blew a raspberry. She folded several arms defiantly, squeezing shut all eight eyes.

Knitbone growled, thinking as quickly and calmly as he could. Moon wouldn't leave Starcross without putting up a fight, not after everything she'd been through, not with Rosabel so close.

"They can't have been gone for long. There still might be a chance of saving Rosabel. Come on – we need to go now!"

"Yes," honked Gabriel. "There's no time to lose, and a lot of ground to cover! Winnie, grab your bike!"

Everybody turned to march out of the orchard. Everybody, that is, except for Orlando, who stayed huddled on the ground, wringing his tail like a damp dishcloth.

"Orlando Pepper!" barked Knitbone, turning around. "Come on!"

"Bad man ghost eez scary. Eez podlob." His voice dropped to a tiny whisper, his eyes as round as saucers and his bottom lip wobbling. "Orlando is afeared."

"Don't be afeared," said Martin, taking his sword from its sheath and slashing it gallantly through the air. "We have to be brave for Moon. Galloping Jasper is a nasty piece of work. Sometimes you just have to do the

right thing, even if it IS frightening. Here,"
he added, taking some pink wafer biscuits out of his utility belt, feeling bad about blaming Orlando earlier. "Have a nibble on these. They are excellent in emergencies."

Valentine reached out his paw affectionately and pulled the little monkey to his feet. "Come on, Orlando, we're all in this together."

Chapter 14

Running Scared

The Beloveds stood in the middle of the lane, darkness hugging them like a cloak. Thick clouds blew out of the east, filling the sky and blotting out the stars. Winnie, sat astride her old bike, took her torch out of her pocket and shone it on their faces.

"Where do we start?" asked Valentine in exasperation. "They could be anywhere. Can't you smell anything with that big nose of yours, Knitbone?"

Knitbone sniffed deeply. All he could smell was helicopter fuel.

"Shhh," hissed Gabriel. "Keep it down; we don't want Jasper to know we're after them."

"Hopefully Moon would try to steer him away from the quickest route," whispered Winnie, stepping backwards onto a twig and making a loud crack.

"SSHHHH!" all the ghosts said. All except for Knitbone, who was having a Sherlock Bones moment.

"Winnie, shine your torch down there."

"Where?"

"On the ground."

Winnie shone a pool of light onto the muddy lane. There lay the twig that she'd trodden on. It was a forked stick with a leaf on one of the prongs.

"The Patteran! Remember?"

Gabriel gasped and slapped his forehead with a wing. "Of course!"

"Clever old Moon!"
woofed Knitbone in admiration.
"She's trying to tell us where she's gone."

Martin inspected the stick. He stood up and pointed his sword in the direction of an open gate. "We need to go that way! Come on!"

They raced through the gateway and into the fields, everyone looking for signs. Animals are naturally good at this sort of thing and it didn't take them long to find another one: a broken branch sticking out of a hedge, and then some crossed sprigs of holly.

"What does holly mean again, Knitbone?" asked Martin, reaching out a hesitant fingertip to touch the spikes.

"Danger."

Orlando crammed his whole mouth full of pink wafer biscuits.

Suddenly Valentine, whose eyes were very sharp, let out a cry. "There! Over there! Look – I can see them!"

The blanket of cloud had thinned to a lacy fleece and starlight had begun to trickle through. In the distance they could see the silhouette of a horse-drawn caravan making slow progress towards the bridge. The horse repeatedly reared up in the shafts and they could hear a furious voice, bellowing and raging. More than once they heard the distinctive crack of a whip.

The ghosts looked at each other fearfully, their bravado evaporating. Orlando was as white as a sheet and had his little hands over his eyes, his teeth chattering like a clockwork toy. Martin had his head between his legs and Valentine and Gabriel were unsuccessfully trying to hide behind Winnie. Time for a pep talk.

Knitbone stuck his tail straight up like a flagpole, his hackles raised.

"Dearest Beloveds," he barked. "We are gathered here today to prevent a great wrong. Do not be afraid! We are fighting-fit phantoms and ready for battle! Remember, it's not the size of the dog in the fight, it's the size of the fight in the dog!"

Whilst everybody tried to figure out what that meant, Knitbone strutted up and down in front of them, as if addressing a tiny army. Meanwhile Orlando hid inside Winnie's pocket with his fingers in his ears, wailing loudly.

"What if you hadn't helped me?" barked Knitbone over Orlando's sobs. "Where would I be now? Remember: a Beloved in need is a friend indeed! This is *OUR* patch, *OUR* Starcross, *OUR* home. How *dare* a strange human ghost think he can come and kidnap our friend! It is, at the very least, extremely rude."

"Well said, comrade!" declared Martin. Fired up by this morale-boosting speech (and several fistfuls of pink wafers), he leaped up onto Knitbone's back, holding onto a tuft of fur and raising his sword.

"Ready or not, here we come," said Valentine, revving up his legs to a blur.

"Knitbone's right. That Galloping Jasper needs a taste of his own medicine," honked Gabriel, as he flapped his great white wings and rose up into the night sky.

Winnie gave her pocketful of quivering monkey a reassuring pat. Then she put one foot on her bike pedal, grabbed the handlebars and narrowed her eyes, ready for the chase.

Knitbone took one last big bite out of a biscuit.

"It's crunch time. Is everyone ready? FOR HEART AND HOME!"

The Spirits of Starcross bellowed as one, surging forward like a tide.

"*CHARGE!*"

Chapter 15

Revenge of the Gibbon-faced Giblet

As they neared the caravan, the Beloveds were met by a formidable sight. A looming figure crouched on the front step, knees bent in long leather boots, thrashing the reins violently. He wore a black velvet coat, high collared and studded with silver buttons. Long and tattered, it flapped in the wind like a demented crow. On his head, perched on top of black curls, was a battered tricorn hat and at his throat was a bunch of torn, grubby lace,

pinned with a silver skull brooch. He wore a leather waistcoat, slashed and patched. In his belt was a catapult, wrought with silver and studded with jewels. From the series of large and savage scars on his face, it was clear that he was no stranger to a fight. To make things worse, he stank of the thing animals feared most of all – fireworks. Moon was right; Galloping Jasper was a Beloved's nightmare.

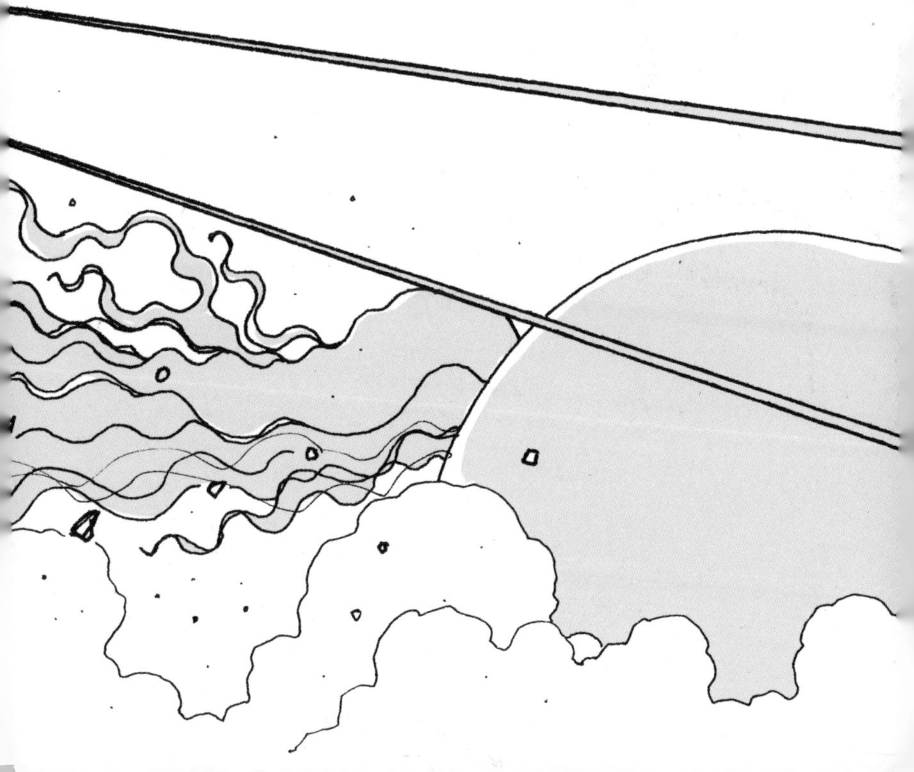

Knitbone growled. Moon was doing her very best to slow their progress, digging her heels into the mud, bravely fighting every step of the way.

Summoning up all his courage, Knitbone stood tall and snarled as boldly as he could, running into the path of the wagon. "Let her go!" he barked. "She doesn't belong to you, Jasper! Moon is a free spirit!"

Jasper waved his catapult at Knitbone in irritation, like he was an annoying fly. "Free? Oh no she's not, she's mine! Blasted Knitbone Pepper," he cursed, glaring at him through his red eye mask. "Be gone or it'll be the boot for you, you dastardly mongrel!" He kicked out at Knitbone, narrowly missing him. As he did so his deep pockets jangled and items of antique jewellery spilled out onto the grass. With a gasp, Winnie recognized them as her mother's. "Never mind, plenty more where that came from," Jasper said and he let out a heartless, hollow laugh, driving the wagon on. "Giddy up, Black Bertha! Not far to go now!"

"Her name is Moon *not* Black Bertha, you kidnapper!" honked Gabriel, swooping down over Jasper's head and peck-peck-pecking at his tricorn hat.

Furious, Jasper loaded his catapult, squinted through one open eye and aimed straight for Gabriel.

"Oh my shivering spoons, he gotta scary pinger!" whimpered Orlando, diving deep down into Winnie's pocket.

"FIRE!" bellowed Jasper.

The silver ball shrieked through the air, piercing the night sky.

Abruptly Gabriel stopped, frozen in mid-air. Looking down at his chest he could see that Jasper had missed, but Gabriel was ready to return the gesture anyway. He streamlined himself, angled downwards and dive-bombed the highwayman. He dropped out of the sky like a stone, nearly knocking Jasper off his perch in the process.

Taking advantage of Jasper's faltering feet, Valentine bounded into a high somersault, flipping and whipping off Jasper's tricorn hat and placing it back on his own head at a rakish angle. Infuriatingly for the highwayman, it suited Valentine's dashing good looks far more.

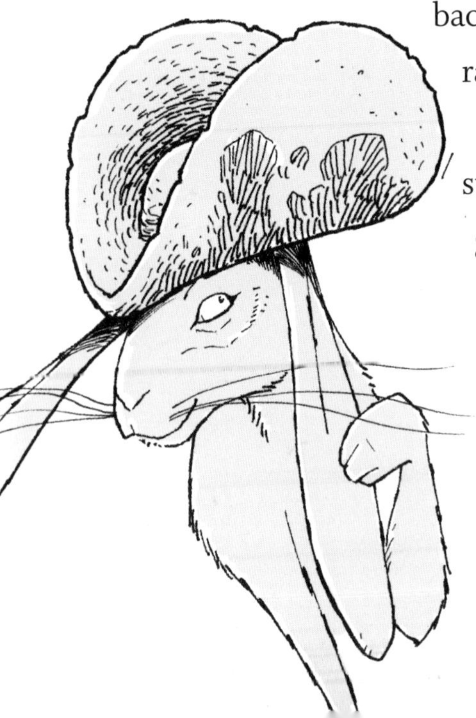

"My hat!" bellowed Jasper, grasping at his naked curls. "A fleabag rabbit stole my hat! It'll be the pot for you, you vermin! You stubble-stag! Give it 'ere!" Valentine raced past the caravan, just out of Jasper's reach.

Distracted and making frantic grabs at the hat, Jasper didn't notice Martin clinging to Knitbone's back. With a devil-may-care leap, Martin jumped up and clung to the side of the caravan like a sticky burr, scaling along the side until he reached Jasper's feet.

Martin had been the Beloved of William Pepper, a little boy who had ambitions to be a soldier. They had spent many happy hours reading war comics together and play-fighting. Consequently, Martin rather liked weapons. He pulled out his sword and stabbed Jasper smartly through the boot.

"Aargh! It's a cussed rat with

a dagger! Forsooth, you are a vile hedge-pig!" yelled Jasper. Peeved by the insult, Martin stabbed him in the other foot too.

"AARRGGHH!" bellowed the highwayman.

Whether it was the pain or the shock, Galloping Jasper dropped the reins and tumbled to the ground, the caravan coming to a grinding halt. Glowing with rage, he staggered to his feet.

"HOW DARE YOU!" he boomed, hopping mad and pointing his catapult at them. "Who do you think you are? You're no match for the likes of me! Listen 'ere, you tatty bunch of bog beasts, I am a HOOOMAN ghost. Do you even know what that means? I'll tell you, shall I? It means that I am *Officially Scary*. I am the *BEST*. Not like you grizzled bunch of ruffian snipes."

Jasper pulled a handkerchief out of his waistcoat pocket to wipe the mud off his doeskin breeches. "Oh, and don't think I haven't heard of you lot neither. The 'famous Spirits of Starcross', the 'Beloveds of Bartonshire'!

"Mistress Jones has told me all about you bunch of muddy-minded maggots. HA! You know what you is? Amateurs! That's what you is! I suggest you go 'ome to your nice dusters and tourists and…and…*wardrobes* and leave the proper haunting to the big boys. You're animals, you ain't as good as people. Get my drift? Understand? Or should I bark or squawk or whinny to make it clearer?"

He prodded Knitbone and Valentine in the chest with a bony finger. "You're giving ghosts a bad name. That big house up there stinks of smiles and sunshine. You're a disgrace. Proper ghosts don't just haunt – we *robs* and we *terrifies*, so you want to watch your spooky 'alf-witted animal selves before I teach you a proper lesson you won't forget for the next thousand years!"

Like most evil villains, Galloping Jasper had a tendency to like the sound of his own voice a bit too much, instead of concentrating on more important things – like how his grand plan was being sabotaged behind his back. For whilst he was ranting, Winnie had calmly clambered onto the side of the caravan and was busy trying to disable the wheels. She put Orlando on the window sill for safety, but he was trembling so much that he fell backwards through the window into the wagon with a tiny squeak.

"Oh yes," Jasper went on, stroking the caravan's paintwork and still not knowing when to shut up. "Good job on the old wagon by the way. You spruced it right up nice and proper, you did." He shook his head and chuckled. "At least your little holiday wasn't completely wasted, eh, Bertha? Especially now I've made it worth my while with a bit of thieving. Ah, the old highwayman habits die hard, they does!" He cracked the whip over Moon's head and gave a cruel cackle.

Knitbone snarled and barked and growled, snapping at Jasper's heels. The highwayman straightened his mask and sneered. "Ahhh, *shut up*, you clay-brained clot-pole," he spat, hauling himself up into the driver's seat, picking up the reins again. He turned and kicked out at Knitbone, narrowly missing his ribcage.

"NO!" shouted Winnie, dashing to protect Knitbone.

“Stop it! STOP it, Jasper! Don’t hurt Knitbone,” Moon whinnied and reared up. “Alright, I surrender! Please leave my friends alone! I feared this would happen.”

She turned her head to look at them in defeat. Her eyes were wild with panic and beads of sweat rolled down her nose like tears.

"Thank you for all you have done for me. Please give my love to Rosabel. Tell her I am sorry. But all is lost."

Jasper rolled his eyes impatiently and huffed. "Lawks, are you still going on about that woman? Everywhere we go, for years and *years* and years, on and on. Listen, it's simple, my name is *Galloping* Jasper – I need a horse!" he said, pinging the elastic on his catapult. "You've got to forget about Rosabel Starr: you's *mine* now, Bertha. I don't know how many times I've had to tell you." He gave a nasty leer, his scars twisting. "She probably wouldn't want you anyway, what with you being so old, and stubborn and—"

A little voice interrupted him. "Oh noes. Oh very dearie me."

Everybody turned to see Orlando leaning in the doorway of the caravan. He had a strange, fixed smile on his face and looked deadly calm. "It would seem, Mister Gallop," he continued politely, "that we have an unfortunate podlob."

Next to Orlando was the box of antique silver spoons. The ghosts looked at each other sideways.

"The thing is," the little monkey continued conversationally, his eyes glittering dangerously,

"Orlando would like to know WHY his special, shiny star spoons are in the back of caravan?"

The highwayman spluttered with laughter, looking around at the others and waving his catapult. "Well, that's a silly question. What are you? Daft in the head? I STOLE 'em o'course, you gibbon-faced giblet! Pretty silver spoons are right up my alley."

This was the biggest single mistake of Galloping Jasper's criminal career.

Orlando – small, strange, and in all likelihood utterly mad – narrowed his eyes to savage little slits. He began to tremble and shake with rage, letting off the most awful, terrible, eye-wateringly, knee-shudderingly dreadful *stonking stink*. The smell floored Jasper in seconds, leaving him writhing on the floor.

Then, not content with knocking out Jasper's nervous system, Orlando proceeded to go c-o-m-p-l-e-t-e-l-y BESERK.

With a shriek that sat somewhere between psychotic peacock and an ambulance siren, Orlando unleashed his inner ninja. He mauled, he kicked, he chopped, he pinched. He slapped, clouted, he walloped, he bit and he battered Jasper.

The others watched Orlando, open-mouthed in amazement. They would have joined in, only Orlando was doing such a good job it hardly seemed polite.

"BAD MAN MUST NEVER TOUCH MONKEY'S SPOONS! DOES BAD MAN UNDERSTAND? THIS IS VERY IMPORTANT. ORLANDO WILL LEARN HIM TO RESPECT OTHER PEOPLE'S SPOONS!"

He swatted, he swiped, he whopped and he whacked. He tickled and he tormented and he terrorized. Orlando was relentless in his quest for justice.

Eventually he calmed down a little,

his breathing slow and ragged. Leering over the highwayman, he tweaked Jasper's nose and hissed into his terrified earhole. "SO. NOW. TELL ORLANDO NICELY WHAT BAD GHOST MUST NEVER TOUCH?"

"M-M-M-MONKEY'S SPOONS," sobbed Jasper, gasping for breath. "I must never touch M-M-MONKEY'S SPOONS!"

Knitbone realized with a wag of victory that Jasper was beaten. Making a mental note never to cross Orlando, he padded over to the little monkey and peeled him off Jasper's face. As transfixing as it had been, nobody likes seeing a highwayman cry.

Jasper scrabbled to his feet, his mask askew and his hair sticking up all over the place.

Winnie jabbed her finger at him. "Serves you right! How dare you kick my dog!" She picked up her old, wonky bicycle. "Here," she said. "This is more your style. On yer bike. And don't EVER think about coming back."

"Naughty ghost wanna watch out!" screeched Orlando, showing the whites of his eyes. "Remember – monkey ever SEE bad man, monkey DO bad things!"

The highwayman quickly mounted the little bike and crouched over the rusty handlebars, his boots slipping and skidding off the pedals.

The bell unexpectedly dinged in a most undignified manner. Confused by the newfangled contraption, Jasper didn't know what to do so, always keen to lend a helping paw, the ghosts gave him a good hard shove down the steep hill.

Trembling and pedalling furiously, his tattered coat flapping behind him, Wobbling Jasper bumped up the starlit potholed lane, never to return.

"Well," woofed Knitbone, licking Orlando affectionately. "You really *are* double-bonkers, aren't you? Remind me never to touch your spoons."

"Oh, Orlando," neighed Moon, turning the caravan around. "You are so brave. You scared a human ghost away. You're my hero!"

On this occasion, everyone had to agree.

"He's left his hat behind too," said Gabriel, whipping it off Valentine's head and throwing it like a frisbee over to Winnie. "It'll be perfect for the invisible section of the exhibition."

They were all busy celebrating and congratulating one another, when Valentine urgently stood up on his hind legs, his ears twitching back and forth. "Hold on, what's that?"

Everyone stopped dead still and listened as the noise got louder.

"Why are there millions of lawn mowers being started up in the courtyard?" asked Martin.

"Lawn mowers? But we haven't got any... Oh NO!" cried Winnie, the realization dawning on her. "It's the helicopter! Rosabel's leaving!"

Chapter 16

Starry Starry Night

Like rockets, everybody shot into the wagon. Moon broke into a full speed gallop, the caravan bumping and jolting along, the spoons jingling and the ghosts and Winnie bouncing around in the darkness like jumping beans.

"Giddy up, Moon! FASTER!" barked Knitbone. Moon's mane streamed backwards in ribbons as the others clung on for dear life.

As they neared the gates, Winnie leaped out.

"Go to the orchard! And light the stove in

the caravan!" she called back over her shoulder as she raced into the courtyard. "Leave Rosabel Starr to me!"

She sprinted over to the helicopter. "Wait!" yelled Winnie over the roar of the blades. "Dr Starr! Don't go yet! Stay for the meteor shower! It's due any time now."

Rosabel opened the window and shouted, "Ah! Winnie Pepper! I had hoped for a chat but I'm afraid I have run out of time." She gave a weary little sigh. "I have a schedule to keep to. So many things to do. Other appointments, you know."

"Please, Rosabel, *please* just stay for a few more minutes," begged Winnie. "I have something very, very important to show you. PLEASE, Rosabel!"

Luckily a lifetime of patiently watching the heavens had made Rosabel Starr both old *and* wise. She hesitated, peering down at the girl. Seeing the desperation in Winnie's eyes, Rosabel turned off the helicopter's engine.

"Alright, a few minutes won't hurt. This thing that you want to show me must be *very* important for you to try so hard. Your parents tell me you are interested in the stars." Rosabel gave a little chuckle and added, "Which does not surprise me at all." She popped open the door and stepped out. "Come on then, young lady. Us astronomers must stick together!" She had an interesting accent, which Winnie couldn't quite place. It was a mysterious mixture of here, there and everywhere.

"So, young lady, is this important thing something to do with the moon?" she smiled. "Or perhaps something to do with the stars?"

"Both!" Winnie beamed in relief. "Thank you, Dr Starr, I promise you won't regret it. Follow me."

They crossed the courtyard, walked around the big hedge and into the orchard. The stars twinkled through the clouds, popping up one by one and bathing everything in starlight.

"It really is remarkable here," said Rosabel, looking up. "No light pollution at all. Most places have light spilling over from somewhere, but Starcross is the same today as it was hundreds of years ago."

"That's very true," Winnie said. "Not many things change here."

"Now is it a special star you want to show me?" said the old lady, skipping over the uneven ground, her warm breath forming white clouds in the cold night air.

"You could say that. I think we've got something that belongs to you," smiled Winnie. "Dr Starr," she said, pointing over to the apple trees, "could you tell me what you can see over there?"

Rosabel peered through the shadows, her eyes adjusting to the darkness. "Well. Now, let's see. It looks a bit like a big box, but there are little lights inside. Maybe it's a shed… No, I think it's a…

OH!" She clutched a hand to her open mouth and hurried over to the caravan, leaving a line of footprints in the frosty grass.

Rosabel placed her hands on the freshly-painted wooden panels, her gnarled fingers tracing the silvery constellations. She looked up at the painted sign, *Moon and the Starrs*.

She turned to Winnie, her eyes round as planets, her face frozen in shock. "My beautiful wagon! Where on earth did you find it?" she whispered. "I thought it was gone for ever!"

"It came here of its own accord," said Winnie truthfully. "One day it wasn't here, and then the next, it simply was."

Rosabel was in a daze. "I searched and searched, for years and years, all over the world…" She rested her cheek on the painted side panel. "Oh, my wonderful old home! My lovely, lovely caravan."

The elderly lady pulled herself up the steps

and climbed inside. "I was born in that bed," she said, shaking her head in wonder and sitting down on a chair. "I saw my first stars out of that window."

She nodded at the glass, frost clinging to its corners like sugar. Rosabel gave a little shiver and moved closer to the black stove, warming her hands in the orange glow, the kindling inside crackling away.

"It's just as special as I remember," she said dreamily. "So many memories; Ma, Pa, my big brothers and sisters." Rosabel smiled to herself. "The nights were always wonderful; polkas in the moonlight, flooding the darkness with bright, beautiful music. Marko's fiddle swooped wildly like a swallow, as Beshli and Kizzy laughed and danced, their bright dresses twirling round and round." Rosabel had a faraway look in her eye. "But they are all gone now. Time changes everything."

She gave a big, heavy sigh and took a photograph out of her pocket. It was black and white, well worn and rather crumpled. She handed it to Winnie. In it was a pretty young woman with her arms draped around the neck of a beautiful white horse. They looked very happy.

"Losing the caravan was bad enough," said Rosabel. "But losing my horse was a thousand times worse. I showed that photograph to everyone I met, in the hope that someone had seen her. I've missed her every day for over seventy years."

She looked up at Winnie. "I'm so sorry, you must be wondering who I am talking about. Moon was my dearest friend and the best horse in all the world." Rosabel looked down at the photograph. "She pulled this wagon faithfully for many years. But one day I made a terrible mistake and I lost my beloved friend for ever. I have never forgiven myself. I should never have left her alone for a moment. If I had my chance again I never would." She fingered the bell around her neck. "But she will never know that. Poor, beautiful Moon."

Rosabel patted Winnie's arm and wiped away a tear. "The caravan is so beautiful, Winnie, and I'm so glad it is at Starcross. But you must keep it. Without Moon it just doesn't feel the same."

"For a while, Starcross felt strange without *my* best friend," said Winnie. "But it doesn't any more."

"Who was your best friend, Winnie?" asked Rosabel gently.

"My dog, Knitbone Pepper."

"Knitbone," said Rosabel, the cogs of her mind turning and clicking. "That is a very unusual name. It's the old word for comfrey, isn't it? Its Latin name means 'to unite'." She looked up, one eyebrow raised, as if trying to make sense of something. "This Knitbone was *your* dog, you say?"

Winnie smiled. "Yes, he is. He was found in the old vegetable garden as a puppy, so he's home-grown; just like me! Knitbone is part of Starcross for ever."

"You must have been broken-hearted to lose him," said Rosabel sympathetically. "These precious companions make such a difference to our lives, but all too quickly they are gone."

"Well, I'm not so sure about that," said Winnie.

Rosabel eyed her curiously and climbed back down the steps by the light of the oil lamps. "Are you saying you don't miss him? This special friend of yours?"

Winnie shrugged. "Actually, no. I don't miss him at all."

Flustered by Winnie's apparent heartlessness, Rosabel didn't know what to say next, so plumped for, "Oh. Right. Well. I see."

"No, I don't think you *do* see," said Winnie

with a smile. "I don't miss him because he's here with me right now."

Rosabel eyed Winnie sharply. She clearly thought the girl was stark-staring bonkers. "Well, I really must be going. Thank you so much for showing me my dear old wagon. I'm so pleased it has found such an interesting home. However, as I said, I have a very busy diary." She looked about her, scanning the orchard. "Now, where's my bag?"

"Rosabel, you're not listening to me," said Winnie impatiently. "You don't have to feel sad about Moon."

"Excuse me, young lady," said Rosabel, sounding very annoyed now. "Just because you don't miss your friend, it doesn't mean that I don't miss mine!" She stood up and hoicked her bag over her shoulder, raising her voice as she got quite worked up. "For your information, I moved to the North Pole to get far, far away from my memories. I shall never be able to forgive myself for losing my horse. Life without her is like a knife in my heart. All the comets and the planets and the shooting stars in the universe cannot begin to make up for the loss of my beloved Moon." She turned to leave, marching over the grass, adjusting her flying hat. She called crossly over her shoulder. "So it would seem that, on this matter, Lady Winifred Pepper, you know nothing."

"Rosabel Starr!" Winnie called after her. "I do know that the silver bell you wear round your neck comes from Moon's bridle."

Rosabel stopped dead in her tracks. Putting her hand to her throat she clasped the tinkling bell that she had worn every day for over seventy years. Slowly, she turned around.

"How could you know that?" she whispered, the realization slowly dawning on her. "In fact, now I come to think about it, *how* did you even know that that was my caravan?"

"Rosabel, you have to trust me," called Winnie.

"I need you to make three wishes, the last one being the thing you want most of all in the world."

"But why?" said Rosabel, walking back to Winnie, her face a picture of bewilderment. "What is going on? Why am I really here, Winnie?"

"Rosabel, please – the wishes. It's truly a matter of life and death."

Rosabel gave a huge sigh, a tired sigh that was full of loss and sadness.

"I wish I understood what was going on," she said, looking up at the caravan. "I wish I could go back to my simple life." She gripped the silver bridle bell to her heart. "But more than these things, more than anything in the universe, I wish…" She closed her eyes tightly. "What I really, really wish is that Moon was here with me now."

As Rosabel opened her eyes again, the clouds parted, revealing the full moon in all its glory.

It flooded brightly down into the orchard. Apples lit up like pale lanterns and the silver stars on the caravan twinkled and shone. It was a wonder to behold.

But none of these could begin to compete with the sight that stood before her: a magnificent shimmering horse, her blue eyes twinkling, luminous in her bone-white beauty.

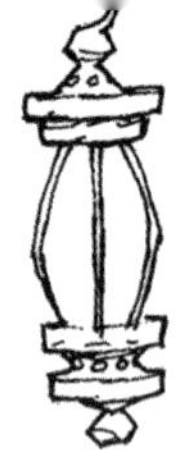

Chapter 17

Straight from the Horse's Mouth

"Moon?" Rosabel stood, frozen to the spot. She gave her eyes a rub and blinked, as if she were seeing things. "Moon Starr?" she whispered. "Is that really you, my old friend?"

Moon whinnied joyfully. "Good evening, Rosabel. I've been waiting for such a long time. I'm so happy you have come home at last."

"Oh my Moon, my wonderful Moon!" Rosabel stumbled over to her, unable to believe her eyes.

She stroked Moon's silken mane in disbelief. "Where have you been? I have been so worried and I am so sorry. Please forgive me, I only left you for a minute, but somehow seventy years have passed."

"Seventy seconds or seventy minutes – you are still my Rosabel," neighed Moon, jingling her silver bells. "There is nothing to forgive. It wasn't your fault."

Rosabel suddenly stopped and stared open-mouthed at Moon. "Did you just SAY something?"

"Yes," neighed Moon joyfully. "And I've got so much to tell you! How, ever since the last moment I saw you, all those years ago, I've been waiting, hoping and wishing that one day we would be together again. How I'd watch the stars, safe in the knowledge that, even though we were apart, you and I might be looking at the same sky." Moon lowered her eyes. "When times were at their worst, when I had nearly given up hope, I would simply search for Pegasus in the night sky and then my heart would feel a little less broken. Oh, Rosabel!" She snuffled her soft velveteen nose over the goggles on top of Rosabel's hat. "Don't cry."

"But these are happy tears," laughed Rosabel. "I'm crying because I have been doing the same! I have such wonderful memories of our old life. Could we go back on the road again, do you think? Back to the simple life? Together?" said Rosabel, the years falling away, her eyes bright. "The helicopter is always breaking down, not like you! I'm fed up of rushing here, there and everywhere. I've been chasing something for so long, and now I've found it." She scratched behind Moon's ears. "Taking the scenic route would be heavenly."

Rosabel turned to Winnie and handed her the helicopter keys. "I won't be needing these any more. I never really liked it. We'll go the old-fashioned way, like generations of Starrs before me. You can't beat a horse for travelling in style."

She wrapped Winnie in a big hug. "I don't understand any of this, but thank you so very, very much, Winnie Pepper of Starcross Hall. You have given us our greatest wish."

"Oh, well," said Winnie, blushing. "Well it's not just me, it's all the others too."

"Others?" asked Rosabel, looking about.

"Yes, Knitbone's here right now – he's my Beloved, like Moon is yours. Then there's Valentine the hare, Gabriel the goose, Orlando the monkey and Martin the hamster. They're all Pepper Beloveds too," Winnie said breezily, as everybody waved.

"Should I be able to see them?" whispered Rosabel behind her hand. "Am I doing something wrong?"

"Oh no," laughed Winnie. "Only I can see them. I think I'm just lucky like that."

Rosabel gave her a broad smile and climbed up into the caravan's driving seat, just like she'd done thousands of times before. As she did, silver sparkles began to pour from the clear October sky, raining down, one glorious ribbon of light at a time. The meteor shower!

Rosabel looked up into the sky, her eyes twinkling. "Here it comes! Perfect travelling weather for Starrs." She was beaming as she picked up the reins, looking as if she would never let them go.

"Goodbye, dearest Beloveds," neighed Moon, looking down at her new friends, her pale blue eyes gazing through soft black eyelashes. "I can't thank you enough. Because of your kindness and bravery, my heart is whole once more. Roojoo was right: you are the truest, bravest friends a ghost could ever hope to have. I will miss you all."

"Farewell, m'lady," said Valentine bowing low, stifling a sniffle.

"The honour has been ours," honked Gabriel, fluttering his wings and pretending he'd got something in his eye. Martin stepped forward with a smart salute and Orlando gave a little curtsy, his bottom lip wobbling uncontrollably. Then he held out the blue plastic owl, the one he'd dug up in the conservatory, as a token of his undying love. "Eez Twit, for yooo."

and the
STARRS

Winnie placed it on the step of the wagon.

Knitbone nosed about in Winnie's pocket for some ginger biscuits and nudged them into Winnie's palm. "You're going to need lots of these too," said Winnie, handing them to Rosabel.

"Goodbye, Moon," whimpered Knitbone, trying hard to wag his tail. "Safe journey. If you see Roojoo again, send him our love. You will come back someday, won't you, if you are ever passing Starcross?"

"We will. Goodbye, Knitbone Pepper," whinnied Moon. "I will never forget you. Thank you for everything."

A tantalizing northern wind whipped up, laced with the familiar perfume of woodsmoke and grass. Moon's hoofs began to dance on the spot and her bells jingled.

"There is just one last thing before we go." Rosabel leaned across to Winnie with a curious smile, her eyes crinkling. "Winifred Clementina

Violet Araminta Pepper, listen carefully to what I am about to say. I meant to give it to you earlier, but in all of the excitement I forgot something rather important. In the glovebox of the helicopter is a gift for you. You see, I have always known that Starcross was special." She gave a chuckle and shook her head ruefully. "But heavens above, I had no idea HOW special."

She blew them a kiss, wrapped her furs about herself and lowered her flying goggles. "Kushti bok, dear friends!" Rosabel let out a powerful wolf whistle and jingled the reins. "Hold onto your hats! Moon – to the open road!"

Moon reared up with a loud whinny, lowered her head into the wind and broke into a jingling canter, her shimmering white mane rippling like a river. As the heavens spilled their dazzling, starry treasures across the sky, Rosabel and Moon raced into the dark velvety night, jingling in time, together once more.

Winnie and the Beloveds stood and waved and waved until they couldn't see them any more. Martin had to stuff a ginger biscuit in Orlando's mouth to drown out the wails.

"Cheer up, Orlando. I'm sure one day they'll be back for a visit," said Knitbone with a forced wag. "You *are* her hero after all."

Orlando gave a little sniffle and kissed one of the spoons. Goodbyes were always such bittersweet affairs.

Chapter 18
Written in the Stars

Winnie popped open the helicopter door and felt about in the glovebox. In it was a parcel wrapped in brown paper and tied with string.

"So, what's in the parcel, Winnie?" woofed Knitbone, as they walked back to the house.

"It definitely feels like a book," she said, weighing it in her hands. "And a big one at that."

"Dr Starr is a scientist, so it's probably a textbook. We can put it in the library. I'm actually very good at science," honked Gabriel knowledgably. "My specialist subject is electrickery."

Valentine shrugged, competitive as ever. "Pooh. Electrickery is old hat. I'm more of an astrofizzicks sort of hare."

Knitbone watched closely as, stars still falling, Winnie sat on the front step of the house and unwrapped the gift. It was indeed a book, with big letters on the front:

"Look, Winnie," said Knitbone. There was a bookmark sticking out of the middle with *Starcross* written on it. Winnie felt for it and opened the book to the correct page. It was headed:

Early Female Astronomers of England
Starcross Hall, Bartonshire

"Well knock me over with a feather! How exciting!" said Gabriel, craning his long neck to see. "Starcross is in a book!"

Martin jumped up and down in excitement. "That's what Rosabel must have meant when she said she knew Starcross was special. Maybe it's to do with one of your ancestors."

Winnie began reading out loud. "*Starcross Hall*," she began, "*has a long history of eccentric aristocrats. None more eccentric than the reclusive Lady Araminta Pepper; astronomer, animal lover and 'magikal herbalist'. Rumoured to be the inventor of the earliest telescope prototype (of which no trace has ever been discovered), the founder of Starcross Hall was light years ahead of her time.*"

Winnie turned the page to see a medieval illustration of a young girl.

1109
Lady Araminta Pepper
and her b'loved hound, Comfrey

Everybody was very quiet for a moment. Winnie looked up at the date above the doorway. "1109 is when Starcross was built…" muttered Winnie, fingering her plaits.

"And isn't Comfrey another name for Knitbone?" whispered Valentine.

"And isn't that the old telescope I dug up in the conservatory?" muttered Knitbone.

"And does anyone else think that book in the drawing looks just like THE book?" murmured Gabriel.

Orlando looked down at the spoon in his hand, stamped with the letters "AP" and gave it a squeeze.

Bright streamers came streaking out of the darkness in a torrent of flashing light. A loud "OOOH!" and "AHHH!" came from the astronomers in the candlelit conservatory.

"Quick! The Northern Taurids are peaking!" cried Winnie, racing up to the attic for the best view.

The Starcross sky was astonishing. It really *was* a night of a billion stars. The clouds had completely disappeared, leaving a blue velvet backcloth, smothered with dazzling sparkles, scattered across the sky and falling like loose sequins.

Winnie and the ghosts sat piled up in the window, eating gingery midnight snacks and watching the spectacular show. Lord and Lady Pepper stood in the courtyard below, holding hands and gazing up at the sky. A canopy of stars had

draped itself over the house, lighting up the whole Estate. The view was heavenly.

Gazing into the night, a question twinkled brightly inside Knitbone's head. He tried to puzzle it out, but it was too hard. So he asked the cleverest person he knew.

"What do you think the picture in Rosabel's book means, Winnie?" asked Knitbone, nibbling his biscuit, the falling stars reflected in his eyes.

Winnie's face was tilted to the sky, lit up by the moonlight. She pondered the question for a while.

"Well, Knitbone, dear old dog, Starcross has always been full of interesting secrets and surprises." She turned around to look at him and ruffled his fur.

She had a beautiful smile on her face, one that reached right up to her eyes and back again. "But then we already knew that, didn't we?"

The ghosts looked at each other and smiled, draping their wings and paws around each other.

"All we really need to know," said Winnie with a big smile, "is that we've got a job to do. And that's to look after each other, for always and for ever, come what may."

"Not forgetting the housework, of course," added Gabriel, rolling his eyes. "*Somebody's* got to do the housework."

Knitbone looked out at the endless shooting stars. "Do you think we should make some wishes?"

"Oh yes!" said Gabriel. "I wish for more books for the library, particularly history ones, with lots of pictures."

"I wish for a new hare-brush," said Valentine.

Martin adjusted his utility belt. "I wish for a new one of these. I think it might be shrinking..."

Orlando closed his eyes tightly shut and grinned. "Orlando wish for new, massive handbag for spoons."

Winnie laughed. "Easy-peasy. I'm going to wish for longer school holidays!"

They all looked at Knitbone, who was very quiet. Orlando put his little head on one side. "What you wish for, woof-face?"

Knitbone Pepper wagged his tail and looked into the faces of his beloved friends, stars raining down in the distance. "Nothing," he barked, his heart brimming. "I've already got everything a dog could ever wish for."

The End

Meet the Author

Claire Barker is an author, even though she has terrible handwriting. When she's not busy doing this, she spends her days wrestling sheep, battling through nettle patches and catching rogue chickens. She used to live on narrowboats but now lives with her delightful family and an assortment of animals on a small, unruly farm in deepest, darkest Devon.

Meet the Illustrator

Ross Collins is the illustrator of over a hundred books, and the author of a dozen more. Some of his books have won shiny prizes which he keeps in a box in Swaziland. The National Theatre's adaptation of his book "The Elephantom" was rather good, with puppets and music and stuff. Ross lives in Glasgow with a strange woman and a stupid dog.

Meet

Knitbone Pepper,

the lovable ghost dog!

Knitbone has made lots of new animal friends since becoming a ghost dog. But his owner, Winnie, is missing him.

Can the ghostly gang come up with a plan in time to help Winnie see Knitbone again?

ISBN 9781474931984

www.usborne.com/fiction

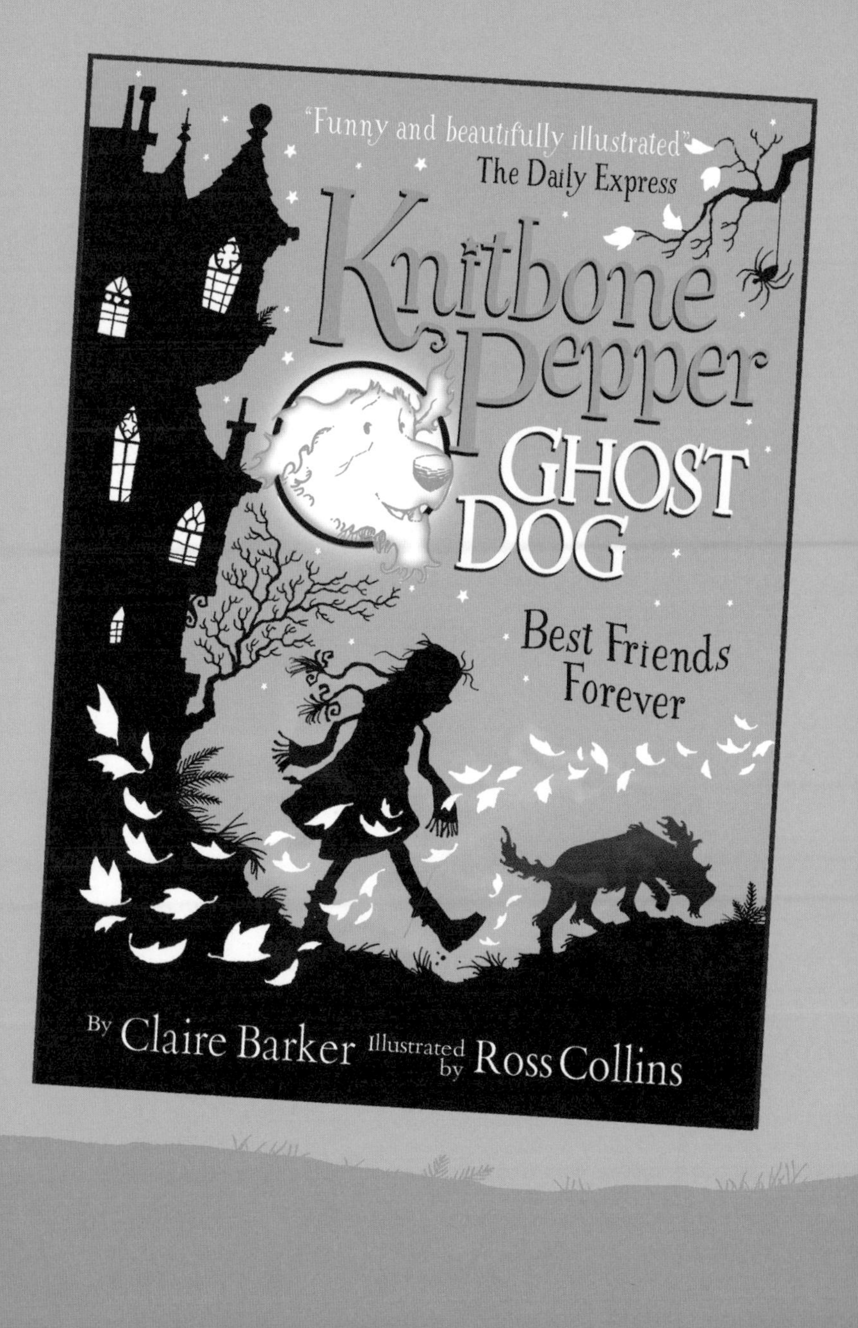
"Funny and beautifully illustrated"
The Daily Express
Knitbone Pepper
GHOST DOG
Best Friends Forever
By Claire Barker Illustrated by Ross Collins

Roll up! Roll up!
The circus is coming
to Starcross!

Winnie and her ghostly
animal friends can't wait!
The magicians, acrobats
and clowns are such fun!

But Knitbone sniffs something
beastly in the big top...

ISBN 9781474931991

www.usborne.com/fiction

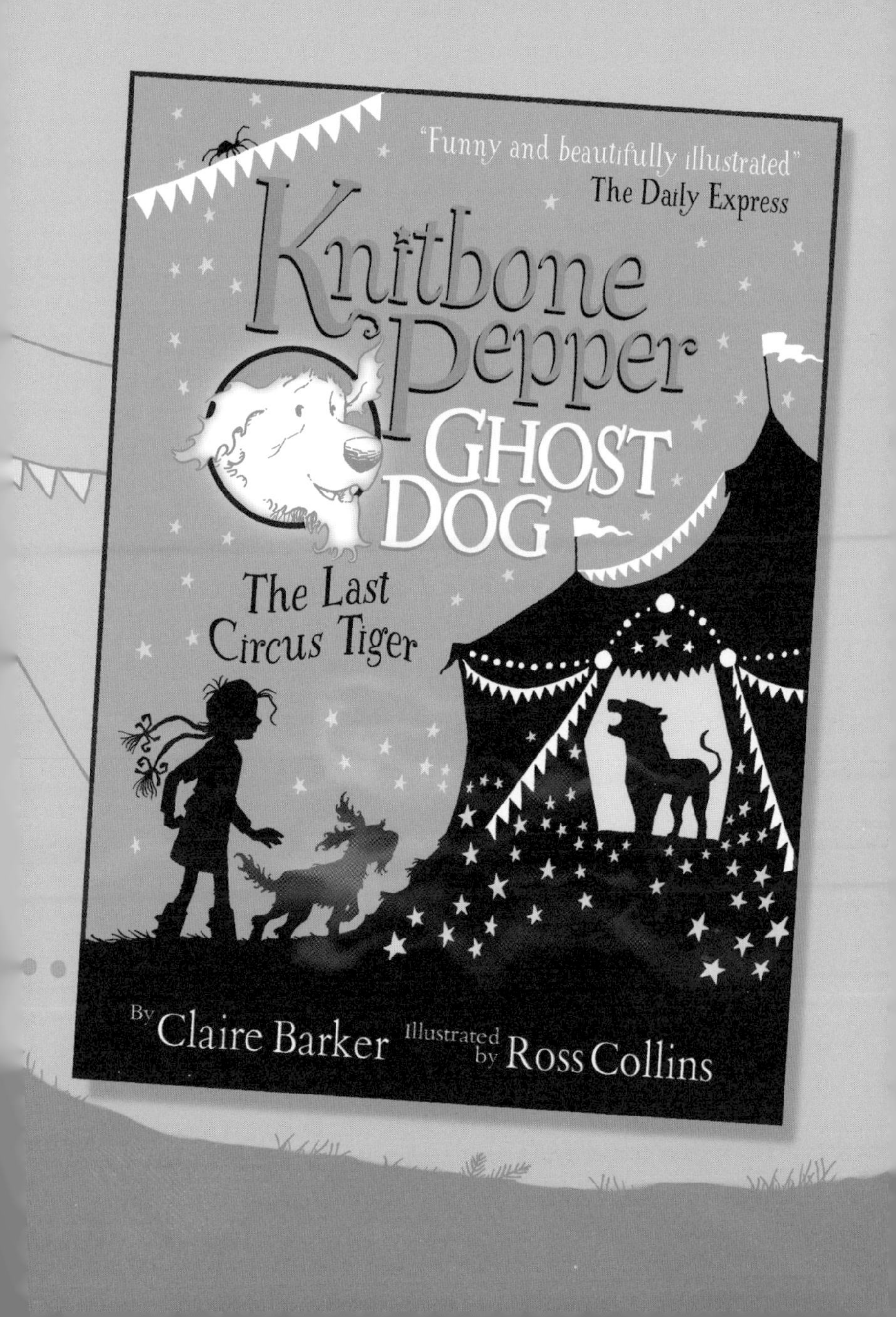
"Funny and beautifully illustrated"
The Daily Express
Knitbone Pepper
GHOST DOG
The Last Circus Tiger
By Claire Barker
Illustrated by Ross Collins

This edition first published in the UK in 2017 by Usborne Publishing Ltd.,
Usborne House, 83-85 Saffron Hill, London EC1N 8RT, England. www.usborne.com

A CIP catalogue record for this book is available from the British Library.

ISBN 9781474932004
Printed in China.